THE
RIVERS
OF JUDAH

CATHERINE FARNES

Greenville, South Carolina

Library of Congress Cataloging-in-Publication Data

Farnes, Catherine, 1964-
    The Rivers of Judah/Catherine Farnes
        p.   cm.
    Summary: Rebekah gradually learns how two different rivers play
significant roles in the life of her friend, Judah, and in her own need to believe
God's promises.
    ISBN 0-89084-864-5
    [1. Christian life—Fiction. 2. Friendship—Fiction.] I. Title.
PZ7.F238265Ri 1996
[Fic]—dc20   94-42661
                                                              CIP
                                                              AC

The Rivers of Judah

Edited by Michelle Pryde
Cover by Mary Ann Lumm
Design by Brannon McAllister

© 1996 Bob Jones University Press
Greenville, South Carolina 29614

All rights reserved
Printed in the United States of America

ISBN 0-89084-864-5

15 14 13 12 11 10 9 8 7 6 5 4 3 2

For my husband John,
my most treasured friend

Contents

Chapter One 1

Chapter Two 7

Chapter Three 11

Chapter Four 15

Chapter Five 21

Chapter Six 23

Chapter Seven 31

Chapter Eight 39

Chapter Nine 45

Chapter Ten 51

Chapter Eleven 55

Chapter Twelve 61

Chapter Thirteen 67

Chapter Fourteen 73

Chapter Fifteen 81

Chapter Sixteen 89

Chapter Seventeen 97

Chapter Eighteen 105

Chapter Nineteen 113

Chapter Twenty 125

Chapter Twenty-One 129

Chapter One

I sat on the steps outside the church to wait for my parents. The sun shone down warm, but the air still pressed like winter at my sweater. Boys and girls dressed for a warmer day dashed by and around me, hurrying to their cars. Adults had stopped in groups to talk, their excitement reinforcing my own.

Ben Ewen. Our new pastor.

It could be different this time.

This man was tough. He had served in foreign missions for seven years. He had pioneered his own church in Alaska, out of which he had built a successful Christian school and sent out eight missionaries. From his rugged features to his quick humor, everything about him said *I intend to do nothing less than stand for the very best God has in store for this church, no matter what the enemy throws at us.*

When he'd said so from the pulpit this morning, I realized that I was a fifteen-year-old, churched-all-my-life Christian who settled for something very much less than the best God had in store for me.

Somehow, though he hadn't quoted any of them, Ben Ewen reminded me of all the Bible promises I had learned about God being in control. Promises I had almost forgotten. And judging by the conversation around me, everyone seemed to feel as confident in our new pastor as I did.

"That man is infuriating!"

Well, maybe not everyone.

I looked up. "Infuriating? Who?"

My sister Elly sat on the step beside me, taking care not to wrinkle her new cotton skirt. Her face was tight with indignation. "Mr. Kramer."

"Oh." I did not want to talk about Mr. Kramer. Our church had two assistant pastors—my father and Joe Kramer. Though the man was a fine speaker, ambitious, and handy at acquiring influence, I didn't like him. He still confused me with Elly—after five years of watching us grow up. Every time he nodded carelessly in my direction saying, "Good morning, Elizabeth," I wanted to hit something. But I had long ago given up correcting him. If he did not know by now that his fellow assistant pastor Rick Cahill had two daughters—only one named Elizabeth—then he never would, and I'd just have to learn not to care. "What did he do now?" I asked, only because I could see that my sister was bursting to tell me.

"It's what he whispered to Mrs. Kramer on their way into the leadership meeting just now." Souring her expression, Elly pressed her chin to her chest in exaggerated contempt. " 'How can Pastor Fenton honestly expect a transplanted hick to minister to sophisticated people?' " She shook her head. "He's just jealous that Pastor Fenton didn't choose him."

I looked away from her at two children who were chasing each other in circles around the lightpost at the corner of the parking lot, and I wished that I knew as little about church politics as they did.

Pastor Fenton, the man who had originally founded our church and had gone on to start several others around the region, had persuaded Ben Ewen to pastor here. It wasn't exactly my idea of the perfect job. In the five years since my father had moved us to Colorado, he had served as assistant under four different pastors. Two of them had been voted out by the board, and the other two had resigned. For the past six months, we'd had *no* pastor.

"You don't know for sure that Mr. Kramer's jealous," I cautioned my sister.

"Sure I do, Rebekah, and so do you."

If I had learned anything from church during the past five years, it was not to get into this type of chitchat. "Well, I don't care what he thinks," I said.

"Then you're stupid." She stood and began walking away.

"Elly," I said, going after her, "he's a big boy. He'll get over it. I mean, he's a church leader. Give him some credit."

Elly stood there on the church steps staring at me, biting her lip. Finally she nodded and said, "Let's go meet Pastor Ewen's kids."

"Good idea." I had seen them sitting on the curb at the far end of the lot with Tony and Michael Kramer and Natalie Potts. "Lead the way."

Pastor Ewen had three kids, teenagers like Elly and me. A daughter and two sons. Even though I hated meeting people with Elly, because she was prettier than me and more outgoing—and often exploited those two facts, I was glad she was with me now. Only someone with my sister's ego and tactlessness could interrupt Michael Kramer if he was talking about Track, which he was.

"Take a breath, Michael," she said, sitting on the curb between the two Ewen boys. She held her hand out to the one on her left—the blond one who was sitting with his elbows on his knees, looking like he'd rather be stuck in a hot car behind road construction. "I'm Elly Cahill," she said. "My dad is one of the assistant pastors." She nodded toward Michael. "Like his father."

Then she glanced at me. "That's my sister."

"Rebekah," I mumbled when the blond boy smiled at me.

"Nathan Ewen," he said.

His sister, petite and fragile-looking like their mother, stood to introduce herself to me. "I'm Rachel."

"And that's Judah." Nathan Ewen looked at his dark-haired brother with the same *It exists so I'd better introduce it* glare that Elly often employed when referring to me.

"Unique name," Elly commented. "I like it."

Judah nodded without looking up at either one of us.

Formalities out of the way, Michael resumed his monologue. A star runner from our town's *other* high school, he loved to recount, in painful detail, the race won in spite of the near stumble in lap two, his vigorous training in the wilderness outside of town where there were no trails and the air was thin, and his three separate victories at last year's state meet.

On. On. On.

I exchanged glances with Natalie Potts. Her father was one of the board members, and as a result of so many pastor-board confrontations in the past we had always gotten along well enough, but we'd never become friends. She raised an eyebrow and sighed.

"I run track." Nathan Ewen squeezed in the comment when Michael stood to demonstrate proper arm positioning during the last four hundred meters of a race.

"I can hold my own in a race." Nathan grinned. "I guess I'll see you on the track."

Tony Kramer chuckled. He was his brother's biggest fan. "You'll see the backs of his shoes."

That did it. From where I was standing, I could see Michael's and Nathan's eyes. They read exactly the same way. *I'll show him.*

There's something to prove here, somewhere, and I'm the man to prove it.

I almost laughed.

Nathan's sister did. Then, while the boys were silent for a moment, pouting, she asked, "Are any of you seniors?"

When Elly and Natalie announced proudly that they were, Rachel grabbed each of them by one hand and dragged them several feet from the boys to discuss their eliteness in private.

"Too bad you couldn't stay with someone to finish out the year," I heard Natalie say. "I'd be upset if I had to start at a new school two months before graduation."

"That doesn't bother me," Rachel said. "I wanted to come with Dad."

"It would bother me," Natalie said.

"This is a big change for our family. It's good for us to be together in it." Rachel smiled. "So, tell me about your school."

As the girls spoke and laughed, Tony and Michael Kramer began debating with Nathan whether the training was more gruesome here or in the untamed regions of Alaska.

I stared at the ground for a few moments, and then at Judah Ewen. He'd been peering into his bulletin this whole time. My sister had put the thing together. It was not that interesting. I sat beside him. "Your dad did great today."

He closed the bulletin, folded it, and smiled at me.

Judah had inherited his father's brown hair, rough features, and overall healthful appearance, but his eyes, blue like Mrs. Ewen's, held none of the tenacity that had been so evident in his father's brown ones.

But then, why should they?

It had to be terrifying, didn't it, leaving behind his friends, his church, his home, his school, and everything else familiar and safe? It had to be unnerving, didn't it, knowing that, wrong or not, people here would be watching him, probing, scrutinizing, and evaluating him, judging and rating his father's competence on the basis of his conduct?

His brother Nathan did not seem to be suffering any attack on *his* confidence, though. That boy was obnoxiously sure of himself. Even his sister Rachel, though in a different and quieter way, carried herself securely. No wadding and unwadding unused tissues or

4

paying undue attention to the position of her clothes. Judah, however, looked about as confident as a cat suddenly aware that he was creeping past a sleeping bulldog. He wasn't trembling, but he wasn't about to make any fast moves, either.

"Are you a junior?" I asked him.

He nodded.

"So am I. Maybe you'll get in a couple of my classes."

When he smiled again, this time like he meant it, I automatically looked away. Nothing cemented my opinion that I was plain and uninspiring—like a windowless garage door—more efficiently than an attractive boy . . . with the possible exception of my sister.

"I don't think you're understanding me, Michael," Nathan Ewen was saying when I glanced around Judah's shoulder at him. "This river that I'm talking about gets so fast and deep that a person can't cross it." He steadied his eyes on Judah with an intensity that made the hair on my arms stand up and turned Judah's fingers white around his yellow bulletin. "Nobody should be doing that alone."

"Nobody should be doing that, period," Judah's sister said suddenly, irritably, interrupting Elly to do it.

I got the feeling that the Ewen kids were discussing much more than the depth and speed of some river in Alaska, but I didn't dare ask what.

"Save the competition for the track, Nathan." Though Rachel had lowered her voice, her eyes remained firm. "Talk about something else."

"She's right," Elly said. "You guys sound like the last board meeting I overheard."

"Hey," Natalie protested, "your father was at that meeting too, you know."

"Ladies," Michael Kramer said, obviously enjoying himself, "let's maintain our manners."

"Listen." Nathan raised his hand in a gesture meant to still everyone. "I guess we're all a little edgy, this being Dad's first time here." He smiled. "Let's hope our parents are getting along better than we are."

"One can only hope," Elly muttered, with a terse glare at Michael that nobody missed.

"I'm sure they are," I said. "I'm going to see if the nursery is picked up." I took three steps away from the group, then turned and spoke to Elly. "You should tell the Ewens about the skit you wrote for youth camp last year."

I walked away knowing that this would turn the conversation silly because that's the kind of skit it was, but wasn't silly preferable to rude and unforgiving?

As I crossed the parking lot I thought about the promise I felt for our church in Pastor Ewen. It was a promise I shouldn't doubt or question because of some unspoken but stomach-twisting tension between Nathan and Judah. I was a teenager. I understood that insecurity often hid in rudeness, and that sibling relationships were rarely flawless. Elly and I proved that adequately enough.

But, perhaps I had expected more from the Ewen kids because their father was a pastor—*the* pastor.

"Perhaps you were a jerk," I mumbled.

I refused to be guilty of that which I hated when it came down on me: that *Pastors' kids better be better or else* attitude. And I determined right there in the parking lot as I passed by Mr. Kramer's big green bomb of a car, that I would not be part of the pressure our church would try to heap on the Ewen kids.

I would fight it with them.

Chapter Two

I inspected the small rainbow-painted room once more before closing the door. The nursery was in order, ready for Wednesday night's round of Dump Every Toy Box.

Quickly, I walked down the hall to the sanctuary. It could probably use a tidy-up too. Bulletins, candy wrappers, tissues, pens, all left behind.

For once, the heavy door didn't squeal when I pushed it open, and I was glad. Judah, who must not have heard me come in, was playing the piano and singing. To three hundred and two empty chairs . . . and me. Recognizing the worship chorus from youth camp, I leaned against the wall to listen to him sing it through once, and then joined him at the piano, singing harmony.

We sounded good together. Anyone would have thought so.

"I didn't hear you walk in," Judah said when we had finished. "I would have quit."

"Why? You sounded great."

He shrugged. "Is it okay that I'm in here?"

"Your dad's the pastor," I replied, smiling. "Go where you please."

His grin disappearing, he tapped the piano bench and said nothing.

"Are you nervous," I asked quickly, "about starting school?"

He shrugged again.

Time hung annoyingly between us for a moment, and neither of us seemed to know what to do with it. Finally, after sitting on the edge of the chair closest to the piano, I said, "So, Judah . . . are you named after someone, or is it just that Judah is a Bible name?"

"For my great-grandfather," he said. "He was a tent preacher."

"A little wishful thinking there?" When he didn't laugh, I hurried into another question. "Do people call you *Jud* for short?"

He cringed as if I had sprayed water at him, then laughed. "Judah's bad enough."

"I like the name."

"Uh huh. What about you? Becky? Becca? Ree-bekah?"

My turn to scrunch up my face. "Just Rebekah, thanks."

Another awkward silence.

This boy's intensity intrigued me. "I heard that this winter was brutal in Alaska," I said, just to say something. "How do people stand it? How did you stand it?"

He stared so acutely at me for so long that I began to wonder what he was looking at—or for. Before looking away, he said, "We weren't in Alaska this winter. We were in Montana with Dad's parents. They have a ranch."

"Didn't you just . . . I thought you guys came here straight from Alaska."

"Nobody said that."

That was true. "Was your father pastoring in Montana?"

"No."

Should I ask Judah Ewen what his father *was* doing up in Montana and why he quit pastoring his church in Alaska before they came here? Definitely not. If I decided that I had to know, I could ask my father later.

"Will they be much longer?"

I laughed. "Who knows. There are men in that room who will want to know your poor father's interpretation of every trumpet and vial in the book of Revelation."

"Dad will love that." After pounding out a few chords of a tune I didn't recognize, he said, "I guess I am nervous about school. See, in Alaska, we went to our church school. You can imagine how that is. Small. Strict. Godly. In Montana, Mom taught us at home." His hands went to the keys again, but he smiled and pulled them back. "I've never been in public school."

"It's . . . different than what you're used to, I'm sure."

"Yeah. I'm sure too. And I want to do right there, you know . . . for God. Like Daniel." He thought for a few seconds. "I've never really had to stand for Him before, being in my father's church school. Here, I guess I'll see what I'm really made of in God."

How had the conversation rerouted itself so quickly from weather and a good book to something that twisted my own insides against me? "You'll do fine," I said coldly.

"You don't know me," he pointed out. "I could be the weakest Christian in the world, for all you know."

"I doubt that."

He squinted at me, obviously confused by the venom in my tone. "No, I mean it," he said. "I could be a terrible friend. You don't know. Don't just stay I'll do fine."

"If you want to serve God, you will."

More poison. More anger. Because I envied his concern. It revealed a commitment to God that I had never fully made. Who was I to preach at him?

Nobody. That's who.

The truth of it stood right in my face, and no amount of sarcasm, or changing the subject, or trying to cover it up by saying all the spiritual things was going to change the fact that I had seen it . . . *was* seeing it . . . or that it was ugly.

"How do kids treat you when you tell them about Jesus?" Judah wanted to know.

How would *he* treat me, I wondered, if I told him that I'd never actually told anyone about Jesus. Sure, I had invited kids to youth group, to Christmas programs, to church. I was pro-life, antidrugs, and vocal about good, clean living, but . . . "Do you really have to ask?"

"I guess not." More pounding on the piano. "It's per-se-cu-tion." He grinned. "Do you get together with other Christian kids before school to pray?"

"Do you want to be a youth leader when you grow up, or what?" My stomach hurt. "What a youth leader-ish thing to say."

"It's a good thing to do, Rebekah. Sometime people need support from other Christians." He quieted his voice. "From friends who'll understand and help out without judging."

"That would be nice," I said, "except, can you really see someone's sin and not think less of him?"

"Everyone's but my own," he answered.

I decided to test that. "So, if I told you I've been a coward about witnessing, what would you tell me?"

Keeping his eyes on mine, he said, "I'd say your half way to fixing it by being honest enough to admit it. Now you have to repent, quit looking back, and move on." He looked down at the piano, touching the keys with his fingers, but not pressing them. "But you've got to believe you're really forgiven before you can do that."

"Okay. But, what would you *think* of me?" I asked. "Really. Not doctrinally."

He laughed. "Truth?"

"Nothing but."

"Okay. I'd think you are a pretty girl with an amazing voice who needs to quit caring so much about what other people think and start witnessing."

The emotions crowding in on me turned my hands cold and my face hot. I felt flattered, convicted, embarrassed, and safe all at once.

"But," Judah said, smiling, "who cares what *I* think?"

Chapter Three

By Friday evening, the Ewens had settled in enough to invite the church leaders—two assistant pastors and ten board members, plus their families—to a barbecue at their house. Located in an almost historic neighborhood, the tall white house welcomed us as warmly as the Ewens did.

Inside, Mrs. Ewen had arranged the rooms functionally to accommodate frequent guests, but not at the expense of her modest elegance. Porcelain dolls, antiques, and home-sewn quilts placed comfortably here and there kept the stylishness of the place unintimidating.

"Rebekah, right?" Pastor Ewen asked me when I held out my plate for one of the hamburgers he was serving. "Cahill? Rick's youngest?"

"Yes."

"Lots of new names to learn," he said.

I smiled. He was doing fine.

"I hear you've been meeting with my kids before school for prayer," he said. "Onion?"

"No, thank you."

"I appreciate that."

Shrugging, I looked at the platter of tomatoes. "They're the ones doing me the favor." I thanked him for the hamburger and joined the other teenagers on the back steps. It occurred to me as we ate together and talked that I already felt as much at ease with the three Ewen kids as I did with any of the other six—and they were kids I had known since I was ten.

After dinner, Rachel invited Elly, Natalie Potts, and me up to her room to look at pictures from Alaska. None of us could resist the chance to see pictures of a place we hadn't been—not to mention boys we hadn't met—or the opportunity to see her room. We followed her through the kitchen, past the dining room, where the adults were laughing about something Pastor Ewen was nearly choking on his lemonade trying to clarify, and up the creakless wood stairs.

Natalie stopped on the landing. "I could sit here for hours."

She was right. The spot was roomy, and gentle evening sunlight warmed it through white lace curtains. In the corner sat a completely furnished Tudor dollhouse.

"You have gorgeous things," I said.

"The dollhouse?" Rachel nodded. "Dad built that for me when I was a baby. Of course, Mom wouldn't let me touch it until I was eleven."

Natalie laughed. "I'd be afraid to touch it now."

"It's sturdy," Rachel said. "Come on." She hurried the rest of the way up the stairs and pushed open the first door on the left.

We crowded in behind her and sat in a circle on her bed. The overstuffed red photo album was obviously one of her treasures. Its pages were labeled and ordered. Pictures of snow, her church, ice, her friends, midday darkness, her school, snow, her house, more snow, family events, and more snow.

While Rachel explained their school curriculum, I glanced around her room. A pale yellow silk rose on her windowsill earned my attention because it opposed the boldness of the otherwise red, black, and white decorating.

"Did a boy give you that rose?" I asked her.

She smiled and nodded.

Natalie peeked over the top of the album. "And?"

Rachel laughed. "Judah gave it to me when we were kids. He felt sorry for me when I forgot the entire second verse to a solo I was singing at church." She picked up the rose, held it against her chin for a moment, then set it back in the windowsill. "Sorry it's not more romantic."

"But it's sweet," my sister said.

"That's why I keep it."

"Speaking of romantic," Natalie half sang, "who's the boy standing between Judah and Nathan next to your dad's Jeep in this picture?" She indicated the photo with her long pearl fingernail. "He's cute. Think he'd like a Colorado pen pal named Nat?"

"His name's Tom Cook," Rachel replied, not looking at the picture. "He was our assistant pastor's son."

After sitting silently while we looked at the last few pages of her album, she stood stiffly and said, "He drowned last June."

"Who?" Elly asked, and then remembered. "I'm sorry. Were you close?"

Rachel did not answer. She turned away from us to return the album to its place in her bottom drawer, and, when she faced us again, she asked, "Why did your last pastor leave?"

Clearly, Tom Cook's death still dug at Rachel. She wanted to talk about something else. Understandable, but why pick church politics?

"He resigned," Natalie said.

"Why?"

"*That* depends on who you talk to," I said quickly, not failing to notice Natalie's glare. "Some disagreement with the board that—"

"*Some* of the board," Natalie corrected.

I sighed, not wanting this conversation, but knowing I was stuck with it. "Enough of the board to keep it always a fight," I said. "It frustrated him, so he quit."

"Well, whose fault was it?" Rachel studied Natalie's tense expression, then added, "Was the board being unreasonable, or the pastor?"

Throat-squeezing silence.

Not because we didn't have opinions. We did. Strong ones. We'd learned, however, not to share them.

"That also depends on who you talk to," I said quietly.

"Okay," Rachel said. "I understand."

Elly stood up and shoved her hands into her back pockets. "Don't worry, though, Rachel. Church rule is they can't vote your dad out for at least six months . . . barring some disastrous sin."

"Who's worried?" I rushed to say. My sister had once again sparked anger in everyone's eyes, and I was once again trying to squelch it. Fast. "Pastor Ewen is great."

"He is." Natalie relaxed enough to smile at Rachel and me. "Just about everyone I've talked to is excited about you guys being here."

Rachel accepted that, and then she suggested that we go back downstairs before the boys ate all the dessert.

No arguments there.

Natalie and Elly stepped out into the hallway first and hurried down the stairs. When I turned to follow them, Rachel called me back.

"Rebekah," she said, "Tommy's death was real hard on my brothers. You're probably better off not mentioning it to them. Not even to tell them you heard about it and you're sorry." She pulled at a speck of lint on her sweater. Even when it fell to the floor, she did not look up at me. "Especially Judah."

Peculiar advice, I thought, but I told her I would comply with it. After all, wasn't she simply trying to protect her brothers? Why should it feel like more than that to me? Like an incomplete riddle?

It shouldn't, I decided, dismissing my uneasiness and curiosity about it into that place in my mind where things are left alone . . . but not forgotten.

Chapter Four

"We'll pick you up at 9:30," Dad said when he dropped Elly and me off at the church for the Saturday night youth meeting. As I tapped his shoulder to thank him for the ride, he reached back and squeezed my hand. "You've been real good about welcoming the Ewen kids, Beck," he said. "Keep it up. I'm sure it helps."

I climbed out of the car. "I hope so."

Elly giggled as we walked toward the church but refused to tell me why until our station wagon was out of the parking lot and halfway up the block. "He's only brave enough to say that because Pastor Ewen's kids can't date till they're eighteen."

"That has nothing to do with it." I elbowed her. "Who told you that?"

"Rachel." A smile crept from her blue eyes into her *Are we just a wee bit in love?* smirk. "Why do you ask?"

"I didn't know, is all."

Elly squinted at the low sun. "Let's see. Which one might you have been thinking of?"

"Be quiet."

"Hmmm. Nathan's cute, but he's kind of brutish, don't you think?"

"Elly, please be quiet."

"I can't remember, Beck. Is it blond hair that you like—because Nathan's definitely got it—or gorgeous brown, like Judah's?" She tilted her head to the left and pretended to think hard. "He's cute, but you never know what he's thinking. I don't like that. Besides," she paused to giggle, "if you marry him, your back yard will be the land of Judah, your kids'll be the tribe, and you'll have to import a pet lion—"

I stopped walking, pulled her around to face me, and glared at her. "Don't tease me. Just because you think nobody's going to date your ugly little sister—"

"Beck, that's not what I meant."

"It's exactly what you meant." I whirled around so quickly that I nearly ran into Rachel.

"Is everything okay?" she asked.

"Peachy." Pushing back hair that had come loose from my braid, I ran past her and Judah up the stairs.

Judah followed me. "Rebekah?"

I stopped at the door to wait for him, laboring to steady myself.

"Are these rotten peaches we're talking about?"

"It's a sister thing, Judah."

"Well, if that's anything like a brother thing, I understand." He shook his head. "Pret-ty rot-ten."

Relaxing, I smiled and asked, "Where is your brother, anyway?"

"He's sick. Picked up that flu that's going around."

I grimaced. I'd had it too. "It's nasty."

Judah nodded as we walked inside.

"What about your sister?" I asked him as we passed by a group of girls on our way to the classroom where we had most of our youth meetings. I almost didn't take time to notice their stares, but decided I might enjoy it. Judah Ewen *was* an attractive boy, and some of these girls, who had always felt better about themselves in my plain presence, had seen him with me a lot lately.

We prayed together every morning. Walked to classes together. Ate lunch together. And we had chosen to work together on a project for government class—Senators Cahill and Ewen and their sure-to-be-unpopular bill regarding tax credits and nonpublic education for Canyon Street High's imitation congress. Judah and I were friends. That's all. But that didn't mean I couldn't be amused by people wondering about us. I stepped half an inch closer to him. "What about Rachel? Do you fight with her?"

"Never," he replied seriously, oblivious to the stares we had inspired. "I stick up for her. She sticks up for me. We never fight."

"That's nice," I said, wishing I still had a relationship like that with someone. Anyone. A year ago my best friend, Allison, had moved to New York to live with her father. We wrote, but it wasn't the same.

The youth pastor walked by us on his way to the podium.

"There are honestly times I think I would have lost it if it weren't for Rachel." Judah sat beside me in the second row. "Rebekah, if I told you something, would you be—?"

"Dave Jacobi."

Judah and I looked up at the same time, surprised and irritated by the interruption. Pastor Dave, our short but tough youth leader, was standing beside Judah's chair, holding his hand practically in Judah's face. They shook hands, spoke for several minutes, and agreed to meet together outside of youth group sometime to get better acquainted.

Judah didn't finish his question when Pastor Dave finally left, and I didn't ask him to.

"What I want us to think about tonight," Pastor Dave said after our less-than-rousing opening chorus, "is our responsibility to our friends as Christian teens. We've talked again and again in here about choices and consequences. What is our responsibility when we see our friend leaning toward a choice that could be harmful to him? Some choices can end up as life or death. We all know that. How far out of our comfort zone are we willing to step for that friend? Let's start answering that by looking at Hebrews 10:23-25."

Pastor Dave spoke for fifty minutes—long for him, and different. Usually, he'd teach for fifteen minutes, either convicting me into despair or boring me to sleep. Tonight's study was different . . . or was *I* different tonight? Either way, his thoughts compelled me.

I had friends who had made mistakes. Christian friends. Had I said enough? Done enough? Did I have a friend who would risk offending me to tell me I was blowing it, or had I chosen only friends who would tell me I was cool no matter what?

Which kind of friend was I?

During the closing prayer, I asked God to teach me to be His kind of friend, and to recognize and treasure my good friends.

When Pastor Dave dismissed us, I glanced at Judah, half expecting a moment of mutual connection. But he was leaning forward, his elbows on his knees, his hands pressed so tightly against the back of his head that his fingers were trembling. He was breathing like someone trying not to throw up.

Rachel, who had been sitting in back with my sister, was at his other side before I could do or say anything, asking him if he was all right. When he said, "Yeah," but shook his head *no,* she placed her hand on his back and asked him if he was going to be sick.

"No," he said.

"Okay. Let's go call Dad to come get us." He nodded, and they hurried out of the room.

"They're in Pastor Ewen's office," Elly told me when I joined the other kids in the entryway several minutes later.

"Thanks," I said.

The light was on in Pastor Ewen's office. I could see it through the crack at the bottom of the door at the end of the unlit hallway. Wondering if now was one of those times that I could and should help, I approached the door and raised my hand to knock.

"How can you sit there and say that?" I heard Judah ask, his voice strained with emotion.

"Because you're wrong, Judah." Rachel sounded as distressed as her brother. "Tommy was not your fault. It was *his* decision."

"Then why don't you march out there and tell that youth leader to tear out every page of the Bible that he read from tonight? Huh? Then I'm okay. Then you can be right."

"Judah, it's not your fault. It's not."

Should I walk away and pretend I had heard nothing? That's what I wanted to do. I felt like a criminal. An intruder on something that belonged to the Ewens alone—and should have stayed that way.

But it had not stayed that way. I had heard.

Before one more word could be spoken and overheard, I knocked at the door. Hard. Four times. "Rachel, it's Rebekah. I just saw your dad pull up." When the door opened, I stepped reluctantly inside. "Is everything okay?"

"We're fighting," Judah said, forcing a smile. "I told you we never do that, didn't I?" He went to Rachel, who was standing with her back to us, fingering the binding of a book. "Rachel, it's okay. I'm okay. I'll tell Dad you're on your way out."

"You're wrong," she said.

"I'm right." He lowered his eyes and walked past me. "See you in the morning, Rebekah."

I nodded.

"Close the door," Rachel said.

I did.

"You overheard us, didn't you?"

So many questions. Why did Judah feel responsible for Tom Cook's death? Was it his fault? Was Rachel sticking up for her little brother when she shouldn't be? Trying to protect him? Her father? Or was Judah innocent?

Did I really want to know?

"Yes," I said. "Enough. I'm sorry."

Lowering herself to her father's chair as if she thought she would break if she touched it too soon, she looked up at me. Her eyes had filled with tears, and she wasn't bothering to hide it. "It wasn't Judah's fault, Tommy's drowning. He thinks it was. Some people blamed him. But . . . he wasn't even there, Rebekah, and he was right not to be."

I sat down. "Okay," I said. "I believe you."

"That easy?"

"Well, I have no reason not to."

"I could tell you the whole story . . . if . . . "

"No, Rachel. It's none of my business."

She smiled. "Thanks for understanding that."

I nodded, understanding also that this information, though in my possession, was not mine to give away. I had seen gossip, especially uninformed gossip, separate too many friends.

Quiet so far, like the first splashes of rain before an afternoon hail storm, speculation about Pastor Ewen's early departure from his pastorate in Alaska had already begun to tickle the ears of some of our board members.

I was not about to add to it.

Judah was my friend, and I intended to keep it that way.

Chapter Five

The next morning at church, I waited nervously at the door for the Ewens. Having no doubt that Rachel would have told Judah about our conversation, I expected him either to avoid me or hang extra close until he trusted me to guard what I knew.

He did neither. He didn't mention it at all, not even to ask me who I had told, if anyone. This confused me, but it comforted me too. Maybe it meant he already knew he could trust me.

Or maybe it only meant that Rachel hadn't told him. That she was protecting him again . . . from me.

Either way, turning it into a nonissue suited me. That's what it was. Other than the fact that Judah still suffered with it, Tom Cook's death had nothing to do with anything here. And it should stay that way. Private. Left alone. Buried.

"Where's your mom?" Elly asked Rachel when she and Judah sat beside her.

"Home with Nathan."

"He's still sick?"

"Yeah." She laughed. "The boy can't even breathe, and you know what he cares about? Getting better in time for the meet this weekend. His first race is against Michael."

"Sounds like Nathan," Elly said, grinning at me.

"I guess their fastest times are close," Rachel said. "Should be a good race."

"Nathan will win," Judah said. "He always wins."

"So does Michael," I reminded him.

"That'll only give Nathan the extra push he needs."

The arrival of the pianist, who led us in an opening hymn, ended our discussion, but not my thinking about it. Pastor Ewen's sermon, however, evicted every thought of the race—as well as most of everything else—from my mind.

God was as real to Pastor Ewen as any of us sitting in his church. No question. Everything he said, and even the things he didn't need to say, made me want that reality for myself.

Something happened after his closing prayer that had not happened in our church since I had been there: nobody moved. Coats stayed on the backs of chairs and Bibles stayed open. The stillness seemed alive, as if I could grasp its power and hold onto it. Something was happening in the silence. The sound of muffled tears and the sight of heads bowed that I had never seen bowed before proved that it wasn't happening to me alone, and that it went beyond Pastor Ewen's ability, no matter how great, to move a congregation with his words and ideas.

But the pianist, without waiting for a nod from his pastor, yanked us out of that silence and into a hastily played closing hymn.

We sang it. Church ended. We went home.

Life kept on.

Midterm exams were upon us.

Someone stole our car stereo.

Judah and I exchanged our first angry words trying to complete the first draft of our bill for government class by its due date.

Nathan recovered, but the track meet was postponed. Rain fell.

Life kept on.

Chapter Six

Wednesday night, I looked across the table at Dad while I hurried to finish my dinner. The past week and a half had been tough for him. He never said anything to me, of course, but I could always tell when one of the people he was counseling wasn't walking in victory. Weariness showed in his eyes.

I poured him a second cup of coffee.

"Thanks, Beck."

Elly and Mom were in the bathroom, perfecting their appearances, so I had Dad to myself. He had always scheduled alone times with Elly and me when he and one of us would hike a trail or go eat ice cream downtown, but these unplanned opportunities meant just as much to me. I never wasted one. "I'm excited about church tonight," I said. "Pastor Ewen's sermons are so . . . real."

Dad studied me through the steam of his coffee.

"Do you like Pastor Ewen, Dad?"

He nodded. "He's a good man for this church. He's got some really good ideas, and his respect for the Scriptures is humbling, almost." He sipped his coffee and smiled. "And, he has an amazing sense of humor. The man sees a laugh in everything."

"His kids are great, too," I said.

Dad got a look on his face that informed me we might not be done discussing that particular statement even though time wouldn't allow a proper dissection of it now. "I'd noticed that you think that," he said.

I wondered *what* he had noticed, exactly, but didn't dare ask. "It's time to leave," I said.

Dad grinned and nodded.

When we arrived at church twenty minutes later, I greeted Judah and some of the other teens and then sat in the second row with my parents. Usually on Wednesday nights I sat with some of the youth group kids, but tonight I wanted to hear the sermon without Michael Kramer's whispered commentaries about it.

After the opening hymn, Pastor Ewen went to the podium and said, "Tonight I want to talk about something that has always been at the forefront of my mind and ministry as a Christian." He paused just long enough to turn our interest to undivided attention. "The Great Commission."

My expectation flattened like a deflating air mattress. Sermons about sharing the gospel always disheartened me. Invariably, the pastor would prove the need for us to witness, urge us to meet it in spite of our foolish self-consciousnesses, pray for an enlargement of our hearts toward the lost, and send us home . . . ashamed, but no more able to impart words of life than we had been before his sermon.

Why didn't they ever tell us *how* to approach someone with the gospel? What to say? Where to start? None of our pastors had elaborated on that aspect of evangelism to us, and that's why I was still reluctant to witness at school.

Or maybe that was just an excuse . . . one of my foolish self-consciousnesses.

Either way, I didn't want to hear another sermon about evangelism. Not even from Pastor Ewen. Unfortunately, I had no choice.

"I'm not going to spend a lot of time tonight telling you that you need to tell others about Christ," Pastor Ewen began. "I think I'm safe in assuming that you all know that."

Very safe, I thought. But I was still skeptical. This probably only meant that he was intending to devote most of his message to the lack of a burden for the lost in too many a Christian's heart.

"Most Christians have a desire to see souls won to Christ," he said.

Okay. Okay. I'm listening! I had to smile. It was as if Pastor Ewen had structured his sermon just for me. But, of course, he hadn't.

He continued, "But many people are either too afraid to step out themselves, or simply don't know how to. That is what I want to address tonight. The 'How To' part of sharing the gospel. What works. What generally doesn't. I am, of course, drawing a lot of this from my own experiences in the mission field and in starting a church, but there are many tools available to equip believers to evangelize, and I'm also going to tell you about some of them."

Pastor Ewen spoke for forty minutes, bringing us to laughter with some examples of what he called zeal without wisdom, and to tears recounting some beautiful conversions he had seen. He concluded by showing us several different witnessing tracts and saying, "The most important thing you can remember is that *you* don't save souls. God does. You throw seed. Maybe you water it. Maybe you get to see fruit. Maybe someone else does. But *God* grants repentance, and *He* saves souls. Remembering this will keep you from getting discouraged when crowds don't fall to their knees to receive Christ around you . . . and from getting proud when they do."

During his closing prayer, I repented for my initial attitude toward his sermon, and asked God to help me be bolder now that I'd learned some ways to recognize and make witnessing opportunities with my unsaved friends at school.

"I'd like to see us . . . uh . . . step out a little more in this area," Pastor Ewen said when he'd finished praying, "as a church. I'm sure many of you actively share the gospel on your own, but I'd like us to consider starting some kind of corporate outreach. In fact . . . " He paused, sounding uncertain for the first time that evening. "May I be a bit impulsive? I realize that most of you have small children to get home to bed, but for any of you who could stay later tonight, maybe we could sit here and toss some ideas around. There are lots of possibilities. Of course, the board and I will make the final decisions, but this church is as much yours as it is ours, and your input would be appreciated. If you can't stay but have some ideas, please call me."

About fifty people stayed after the closing hymn, including most of the board members and their families, the Kramers, my family, and Mrs. Ewen and the Ewen kids.

Pastor Ewen presented his first idea.

One of the board members objected to it.

Someone had another suggestion.

Six reasons why it wouldn't work.

A third possibility. A fourth. A fifth.

On the foreign field, maybe, but not here.

Pastor Ewen had another thought.

Nope. This church wasn't into that.

Door-to-door witnessing. A booth at the fair. Passing out tracts. Street or mall evangelism. An Easter dinner at the church. Skits in the park. No matter what the suggestion, someone—usually one of three particular board members—opposed it.

Finally, Mr. Cox, our church's oldest—in age and tenure—board member, said, "I think your ideas are a little too outspoken for us, Pastor. True, Jesus said we are to be lights in the world, but must we really be floodlights?"

Michael Kramer laughed and muttered, "I wonder if he made that up himself or if he read it somewhere."

Mr. Cox must have heard Michael, but he went on talking as if he had not. "Our lives speak louder than anything else. As far as Joe Unsaved on the street is concerned, we might be all talk and no walk, as they say, and he has no way of knowing. But people who know us . . . *there's* the open door."

"You're right to a point," Pastor Ewen said, "but the power of the gospel is adequate on its own to—"

"Yes, yes, yes, of course it is," Mr. Cox said, impatiently waving his hand. "But, Pastor, some of the methods you mentioned are, well, flat-out offensive and they harden more people than they save."

Several men agreed.

"Perhaps you have a suggestion, Mr. Cox?" Dad asked. Frustration was evident in his posture and in the way his hand had tightened around the notepad he was holding.

"Well," said Mr. Cox, "I feel that if we live the kind of life that Christ has called us to live, people will see it and will want it. They'll come to us. That's—"

"That's the *Sit ye in your easy chair and preach the gospel to every creature that asks you to* commission," Judah interjected.

I laughed with many of the teens, a couple of adults, and Mr. Cox, but everyone else, including my father and Pastor Ewen, stiffened. Judah's mother began fanning herself with a folded bulletin as his father said, "Thank you, son," with the slightest hint of *no more contributions, please* in his emphasis of the word *son.*

But after studying the angry expressions on the faces of the men around him, and glancing not quite up at his father, Judah looked directly at Mr. Cox—who was still chuckling—and said, "I'm sorry, sir. I didn't mean to be disrespectful."

"Oh, of course you did, young man," Mr. Cox said, waving his hand as if shooing a fly to dismiss Judah's apology. "Quite all right."

Unfortunately, even though Mr. Cox himself seemed more amused than offended, Judah's remark had been anything but "quite all right" by most of the men in the room; they remained brick-faced throughout the rest of the meeting.

To close the meeting, Pastor Ewen assured the laypeople who had stayed that he and the board would continue discussions at future meetings, thanked them for coming, and prayed. When he finished, he stepped down from the platform, spoke briefly with my father and Mr. Kramer, and then approached Judah, whispered something to him, and left the sanctuary with him.

"Uh oh," Elly whispered. She slid over two chairs to sit by me. "Lecture time."

I nodded.

"What an obnoxious comment. 'Sit ye in your easy chair.' " She giggled. "What he was trying to say was probably true enough, but . . . poor Mr. Cox."

I did not defend Judah. Elly would certainly take it as a declaration of devotion to him, and I didn't want to find myself anywhere near the temptation to wind her gorgeous red hair around her perfect little neck and pull until her cute little face turned blue to match her eyes.

Besides, she was right. Judah's point had no doubt been lost on those who were offended by the way he had chosen to make it—and to whom.

"You like him, don't you, Beck?"

So much for avoiding temptation. "Don't start, Elly."

"No." She rested her hand on my shoulder and waited for me to look at her. "I'm serious. You like him."

"I haven't thought about it, okay? We're friends."

"You like him. And you know what? I've been watching, and I don't think it's a one-way thing." She winked and stood up, and then offered her chair to Judah, who had just arrived at the end of our row. "See you later," she said, and walked away.

Judah sat next to me, but before he could say anything, his father stepped in beside him and clasped his shoulder. One of those *Yeah, son, you made a mistake, but I still love you* grips. Though Judah received it with a relieved smile, he remained tense and distant.

"Do you want to talk?" I asked him when Pastor Ewen had gone.

"I shouldn't have said anything."

"My father always tells me to look at these kinds of things as lessons learned," I said. "It's okay."

His hand dug in his pocket but came out empty.

"Anyway," I said, hoping to encourage him, "Mr. Cox got a kick out of it. He loves a good one-liner and some nerve. He probably regrets not having a comeback for you."

"Rebekah," he said, "do you think people won't want Dad as pastor on account of what . . . on account of me?"

I could have laughed, but I did not. He was serious. Too serious. "Don't put that kind of burden on yourself."

"It happens."

"I know it happens. What pastor's kid doesn't?"

We had all heard about the rebellious teen who had disqualified his or her father. Drugs. Pregnancy. Running away. But I could not imagine Pastor Ewen threatening Judah with the possibility.

No.

I realized, somewhat irritated by it, that Judah was a blame taker. "Give us some credit, Judah. We'd have to be brainless to toss out a pastor like your dad because of a nothing thing like what you said." I reached out and straightened his red tie. "Trust me?"

He nodded. "Thanks, Rebekah."

When he left to help Pastor Dave stack chairs so the carpets could be cleaned, I glanced across the aisle at his parents. Mrs. Ewen had stepped in close to her husband, fitting perfectly there. She possessed that rare beauty that was both sophisticated and natural. I realized then that I admired her. Her soft yet confident speech. Her obvious commitment to her family. Her evident strength of character, and the way she kept it gentle.

I watched the Ewens until they left, then leaned back in my chair to wait for my parents, who always locked up after Wednesday night services. The sanctuary emptied while I sat there, and someone reached in to push down the light switches.

Dad must think I'm already outside with Mom and Elly, I thought. Wanting to catch him before he locked me inside the church, I stood quickly and hurried toward the entryway.

Then I heard him ask someone, "Is something on your mind?"

"How much do you know about our Pastor Ewen, Rick?"

I quickened my pace. I did not want to overhear another conversation, especially one that began like that. But I failed to reach the entryway before Mr. Kramer continued.

"What happened at his other church to make him available to come here? Why was he in Montana instead of at his church?"

"I can't say, Joe," Dad said.

"Can't? Or won't?"

Dad sighed. "You know everything I know."

"It doesn't bother you, Rick? His secrecy?"

"If Pastor Fenton has confidence in him, then—"

"I had a huge problem with his attitude tonight," Mrs. Kramer put in. "It's almost as if he's implying that we're less Christian than he is because we don't want to . . . to leave tracts and invitations to church in public restrooms."

Pastor Ewen had neither said nor implied anything like that. The Kramers' overreaction annoyed me. My anger convinced me to listen, and listen well; I stopped walking and sat down.

"And his *kid*," Mr. Kramer blurted. "No respect whatsoever for the fact that he was speaking to a member of the board of this church. Rude is what he is."

This felt like a personal insult. My hands tightened around the back of the chair in front of me.

"Judah knows he made a mistake, Joe," Dad said slowly. "That's why he apologized."

"An apology doesn't change the fact."

"You're coming down too hard on something too small," Dad said. "Why?"

Silence from Mr. Kramer.

"Joe, go talk to Ben. He's our pastor. I'll go with you if it'll help, but you need to understand that until there's good reason not to, I have confidence in Ben."

"That's all fine and good," Mrs. Kramer said, "but the man can't just stroll in here like he's God Himself and expect to change everything. He should have discussed his ideas with the leadership alone first. Maybe we don't want an organized church outreach."

"I can't see why we wouldn't," Dad said.

What could they say to that? The entryway was silent again.

"You think it's okay, then," Mr. Kramer said, "his punk kid mouthing off to Mr. Cox, of all people?"

Dad sighed again. Louder. "No, I don't. Ben doesn't. Judah spoke up when he shouldn't have because he felt that Mr. Cox's position was . . . inconsistent with Scripture."

"Even if it was, that—"

"Come on, Joe. Judah apparently has convictions about witnessing. Good ones, I'd say. He made a poor choice of words, yes. A kid choice. And he apologized, didn't he?"

"He should take more care," Mr. Kramer said.

"That's fair," Dad agreed. "I'm sure tonight's experience will be lesson enough of that."

"I just don't know, Rick." This came after a long silence and sounded almost sincere. "Why were they in Montana? Why'd he leave his church? What's he running from?"

Dad said simply but emphatically, "Go talk to Ben. Handle your concern properly."

"I only want what's best for the church." Mr. Kramer had reduced the animosity in his tone, but not the indignation—some of which was now aimed at Dad. "You know that."

"Of course."

Of course.

"Poor Ben," Dad said to me when the Kramers had gone and I admitted I had overheard them. "I think his road here is about to develop some serious potholes."

Chapter Seven

Destructive, ugly, and tiresome, Dad's predicted potholes began to appear. Mr. Kramer and his growing band of followers, united by "concern" for the church and their "obligation" to preserve us from Pastor Ewen's "clearly significant secret," had begun their back-door politicking. From one legitimate question—Why had Pastor Ewen left his church in Alaska?—they built an attack of speculation.

They questioned everything about the Ewens, to the extent of one of them theorizing that Judah's name revealed his father's conviction that the boy was destined to be one of Revelation's two witnesses. In all seriousness! How the man had concocted *that* bit of insight, I'd never know, but the absurdity of it amused and disturbed me.

Most of the people in our church adored Pastor Ewen, but these dissatisfied few made it seem like everyone was against him.

"Why doesn't Pastor Ewen just tell them what they want to know?" I asked Dad one night at dinner. "They're going after him about every little thing, but they really only want one thing."

As she helped herself to more carrots, Mom frowned and looked at Dad.

"Ask yourself this, Beck," Dad said. "Is he doing a good job?"

"Yes."

"You've seen him out of the pulpit. Do you think he's genuine?"

"Yeah."

"Has he offended you?"

"No."

Dad steadied his eyes on mine. "Then why do you want to know how come he left his other church?"

"Well, *I* don't really care, but—"

He smiled. So did Mom. "Okay," he said, "the people who do want to know. Why do you think they do?"

I shrugged. "Curious?"

"Maybe. Anything else?"

"They think it's something bad."

"Do you think Pastor Fenton knows?"

"I'm sure he does."

"But Dad," Elly put in, "we have a right to—"

"Do we?"

Slowly, Elly lowered her fork to her plate. "Yes."

"I don't think we do," Dad said. "Not always."

"How can we trust him when he's keeping secrets?"

Dad leaned toward her until his stomach touched the table. "Elly, he's said it was for the best interests of his church and family. It's personal. Pastor Fenton is confident it won't hurt us here, so why do we need to know details?"

"It *is* hurting us here," Elly protested.

"Is it? Or are we?" He leaned back again and placed his napkin over his unfinished dinner. "Maybe we've lost *his* trust. Maybe he thinks we'll handle it wrong—the same way all the ridiculous little things have been handled. Like weapons."

"But Dad, if he's done some big sin, shouldn't we at least have—"

Dad closed his eyes. I knew he was fighting a battle of his own about this. "Why," he said quietly, "must we automatically assume that because the man isn't announcing it from the roof of the church building, it has to be some perverted sin? Isn't it just as likely that it was a disagreement with an uncompromising board over something he was probably right about? We've certainly seen that around here more than once."

"So why doesn't he say so?"

"Because then we'd demand to know what about."

"Which definitely isn't our business," Mom said.

Elly did not ask any more questions, but I knew she hadn't settled it in her mind. Like her, I wondered how much I could really trust a pastor who deliberately kept part of himself unapproachable. But, like Dad, I understood Pastor Ewen's need for privacy. Also like Dad, I decided to place my confidence in Pastor Fenton's respect for our pastor, as well as in Pastor Ewen's testimony and service here and now.

He was an extraordinary pastor. His level of personal godliness and his commitment to the things he believed God had called him to were evident in everything he said in and away from the pulpit.

And he was likable. A real person. Direct, straightforward, and *funny*. Church attendance had increased since his arrival. The people liked him.

But the leadership . . . they wrestled violently concerning him.

Adding to the disquiet, especially that between Pastor Ewen and Mr. Kramer, was the competition between their sons. Nathan and Michael had met on the track four times, Nathan winning three races, and Michael one. Michael's victory had occurred at the state meet, though, and he'd run a faster time, so Michael considered the score even and still in need of settling.

And beneath the increasing heat, at the center of the controversy, stood Judah, whose comment to Mr. Cox seemed to have ignited it all. He had apologized to the board, but some of them had not let up—not on Judah, nor on Pastor Ewen's ideas about evangelism.

It seemed that church, rather than school, was going to be the place where Judah would learn what he was really made of in God.

In both places, it was obvious to me, he was made of a lot. The adversity at church seemed to nourish his determination to outshine and outlast it, and to stand firm in what he knew God wanted from him in response to it. At school, his constant character earned him a nickname he hated—Jud Buddha—and had opened several opportunities for him to tell kids about the reality of Jesus. He wasted none of these opportunities, and three of them had resulted in the person's acceptance of Christ. People knew they could talk to Judah, and count on him; so he became a sought-after friend at Canyon Street High. But when he was the one needing encouragement, he turned to only one person . . . me.

Frequently, girls would ask if he and I were dating. Always, though with regret since I had prayed and prayed for a boyfriend like him, I'd explain Pastor Ewen's dating rule. "Yes," I'd invariably end up saying, "it's strict, but think about its benefits: simplicity and reality. Plus maturity in our friendship, not to mention integrity and purity." I'd only learned to appreciate these benefits after hours of whining to God about the situation, but they didn't need to know that. What they *did* need to know was that the dating rule applied to everyone, not just to plain Rebekah Cahill, which I'd always point out. Along with the appropriate amount of possessiveness in my tone for the particular girl asking, this usually put forth more than enough of the point.

Even to me, though, Judah rarely spoke of the pain he felt at being the perceived cause of his father's predicament. But I knew he was hurting—more than I could understand or remedy.

But I tried. By praying with him, and for him on my own. By listening whenever he did want to talk. By suggesting plenty of diversions, keeping him thinking about other things. By doing fun things for him . . . like planning a surprise party on his birthday.

"Where did you tell Judah we were taking him?" I asked Jeremy Aarons as he turned his red pickup truck into the Ewens' gravel driveway. It was Monday, May 26, and I had put Jeremy in charge of developing a suitable excuse to get Judah out of his house so that we could take him to *my* house where everyone else was waiting for us.

"Out for his birthday," Jeremy said.

"The Creativity of the Year award is yours for sure," I said with a laugh. "Jeremy, how . . . uninspired."

"I didn't want to lie to him. He hates that."

I smiled. "He wouldn't get upset about that kind of lie."

"A lie is a lie is a lie. He said that to me yesterday when I told him about . . . never mind."

Sometimes, even though I knew better, I had to wonder if Jeremy knew Judah as well as I did.

"Go get him." Jeremy leaned across me to open my door. "People are waiting."

As I climbed out of the truck, I smiled again. Who would have thought several weeks ago, when Jeremy and Judah met the way they had, that we three would be so inseparable now?

Tall, blond, and flawlessly fit from his pursuit of every tennis trophy available to a teenager, Jeremy Aarons had been shamelessly idolized at Canyon Street High. He had invited me to a party at his house, and I had intended to be there no matter what it took. But the day after Pastor Ewen's first service, when Jeremy sat beside me in the cafeteria to finalize the party details, I had changed my mind.

"Jeremy," I had said, "I decided I don't want to lie to my father. And even if that didn't bother me, I don't want to be part of that environment right now. I can't be if I'm going to claim to be a Christian."

He had laughed. "So don't claim to be a Christian."

"I *am* a Christian, Jeremy."

I am a Christian.

As expected, Jeremy had laughed again. But only for a minute. Judah had put his tray down beside Jeremy's and was standing there, staring down at him.

"You shouldn't laugh just because you can't understand," he'd said. "Do you know what it means, being a Christian?" Before Jeremy could reply or walk away, Judah sat down and told him exactly what it meant.

Just like that.

"If you ever want us to pray with you," Judah had concluded, "after you've weighed it out, let me know."

Predictably, Jeremy's face had gone totally unfriendly, and his comment as he left our table reflected it.

Glancing for the first time at the food on his tray, Judah had said, "We'll have to remember to pray for him."

"Uh huh," I had muttered, unwilling to diminish Judah's vision with the facts. Jeremy Aarons seeing his need for Jesus? No way. Let Judah dream. He'd find out soon enough.

Right.

If every dream marched into the real world the way Jeremy had approached us two weeks later to pray with him for salvation, the streets would be full of millionaires and horses.

Now, after five weeks and several hours together over a new believer's study workbook, Jeremy, Judah, and I were the three at school to avoid if you didn't want to address the possibility that there was a God and that you did need Him.

And now we're the three holding up the party, I thought as I knocked on the Ewens' front door. No answer. Had Judah suspected our plan and found a way to stay late at school? I knocked again. When the door opened a few seconds later, I wished I had not persisted.

"Pastor Ewen?" I said, gazing at him with concern. Judah had mentioned at school that his father had come down with the flu, but the man looked as if he'd had it for weeks already and wasn't going to survive.

"Come in, Rebekah," he said. "Judah went to get Esther at the Benantis'. He'll be back in a minute." He held the door for me, then leaned against it after he'd pushed it shut.

I grabbed his arm and led him toward the couch. "Come sit down," I said. The heat through his sweatshirt frightened me.

"Before I fall down?" He smiled.

"Exactly."

He sat heavily, leaned his head back, and closed his eyes. "At least after this we'll have all had the thing," he said.

I nodded. This sickness had spared none of the Ewens. Judah had come to school with it in order to help me present our bill to the congress of our peers. He'd been shaky and a little pale, but nothing like his father was now.

The door opened behind me, and Mrs. Ewen pushed her way inside, carrying a small bag of groceries, a jug of orange juice, her Bible, and a loved-nearly-to-destruction furry blue puppet. After Judah had taken them from her and disappeared into the kitchen, she greeted me with a quick hug and a smile. Then she looked past me at her husband.

"How's Lori?" he asked her.

Crossing the room to sit beside him, she said, "She's better than you, Ben." She frowned when she kissed his forehead. "I should have been here."

"I don't have twin four-year-olds and a baby to take care of." He laughed, then leaned forward, coughing. "Did they like Mr. Furrylips as much as our kids did?"

"The name is Edmund," Judah said in a squeaky voice, tossing the blue puppet into the small basket of toys next to the door. "Mom, are you sure you don't want me to stay?"

"Judah, it's your birthday." Pastor Ewen stood and walked to the stairs, placing his hand on every available piece of furniture along the way. "Go have fun."

"I'll help you upstairs first," Judah said.

"Good idea," Mrs. Ewen and I mumbled simultaneously.

I watched Judah and his father until they passed Rachel's dollhouse, then turned to Mrs. Ewen. "He'll be okay," I said.

Hugging the afghan she had just folded, she nodded.

Seeing the weariness in her eyes, and how ready they seemed for tears, I sat beside her, feeling about as useful as a bag of birdseed. "Mrs. Ewen . . ."

"I'm just tired, Rebekah." She smiled. "This flu . . . on top of everything else since we got here."

Everything else. Controversy. Rumors. Speculation.

I understood. But what could I say?

"I'm glad you're here for my kids," she said, leaning toward me. "You'll be at your house?"

I nodded.

Mrs. Ewen started to say something else, but she stopped, hearing Judah on the stairs. "Have fun," she whispered.

"We will," I whispered back, standing to meet Judah.

And we did.

Judah was so preoccupied when we arrived at my house, probably by his father's illness, that he acted more confused than surprised when the twenty people in my den jumped up to shout "Happy Birthday!"—until Rachel stepped forward, propped a party hat on his head, and wished him a happy and fun seventeen.

Chapter Eight

After school the next day, I plopped my book bag down by the front door, strolled into the kitchen, and poured myself a glass of orange juice. "Hi, Mom. Mrs. Ewen. How's Pastor Ewen?"

Mrs. Ewen glanced up from her sewing. "He's still a little feverish, but nothing like yesterday. He's been up working on tomorrow night's sermon."

"Good." I lifted a pile of pattern envelopes from the chair nearest Mom, spilled them onto the counter, and sat down. "What are you sewing?"

"Baby clothes," Mom said. "For Sara Dunn's shower. They found out for sure she's having a boy."

As I sipped my juice, I watched Mrs. Ewen. Why would she bother to make anything for Sara Dunn's baby? Mr. Dunn, one of the first board members to attach himself to Mr. Kramer's position, was outspoken, sarcastic, and rude whenever he addressed Pastor Ewen. "So," he would say, "did you just abandon your old church, or did they vote you out because of your disrespectful kids?" Yet, here sat Mrs. Ewen, laboring over a tiny outfit for his soon-to-arrive son. Why not buy the woman a package of diaper pins and the noisiest baby toy available, I wondered.

Elly sauntered in, twirling her purse. "Jeremy and Judah are here, Beck," she announced. She stayed behind me like a disobedient shadow as I walked toward the front door to greet them.

"We're going to the park for some tennis and then to eat somewhere." Jeremy pushed Judah inside and entered behind him. "Want to come?"

"I'd love to," Elly stepped in front of me to reply. "Thanks for the invite."

We got permission, squeezed to fit on the bench seat of Jeremy's pickup, and rode to the park in uncomfortable silence. I felt strangely put out by my sister. She had never wanted to spend time with Judah, Jeremy, and me before. Why now? What was afoot in her little mind? More than finding something to do on a Tuesday afternoon, I was certain.

Bristly grass pricked my toes as we walked toward the tennis courts. Judah and Jeremy claimed one, and Elly and I lounged in the shade of a nearby tree to watch. Swing chains clanged behind us. Children laughed and played. A dog barked. And somewhere a sprinkler was going. Usually, when I came alone to watch Judah and Jeremy play, every point captivated me. Though Jeremy almost always won, Judah played fiercely enough to challenge him—and thrill me. Today, however, my attention kept wandering.

Tak tak tak. The sprinkler kept going.

"Don't you think it's weird that Judah hasn't told you why his father left his church?"

So that's what she's after. "Elly, it's none of my business."

"Oh, come off it, Miss Innocent," Elly snapped. "Dad might buy your 'I don't really care,' but I don't. You want to know as much as the rest of us."

"That doesn't make it my business."

"To me, the fact that Judah hasn't told you makes it more suspicious. You two are close."

"Doesn't anyone in this church have a life of his own to talk about?"

Elly glared at me. "Well, you explain it, then."

"Maybe Judah doesn't know."

"He knows."

"Maybe there isn't anything to tell."

"Beck, pastors don't quit for no reason."

I turned away from her to look at Judah. He was leaping to hit a ball coming at him well above his head. I had told him to give us some credit. Nobody would dislike Pastor Ewen because of his comment to Mr. Cox. Wrong. I had thought that at least our family stood behind the Ewens. Wrong again.

"Elly, maybe we just don't need to know. Like Dad says. Maybe Pastor Ewen burned out. Maybe he got sick of living in Alaska. Maybe they voted him out because he stood for his family's privacy there too. You know Pastor Ewen. He's a good pastor. A good person, period. Maybe people in Alaska are just as good as we are at turning maybes into scandals."

Elly looked at me sincerely, compassionately. "*Maybe* Pastor Ewen should clear up all the maybes."

"Maybe," I conceded.

"Have you asked Judah?"

I shook my head and tugged at a blade of grass.

"Why not?"

"Because I don't want him to think I'm against him. He's got enough people against him, Elly. He trusts me. I don't want to lose that. Why don't you ask Rachel? You two are friends."

"I did."

"And?"

"Personal reasons."

I nodded. "Exactly. Why can't that be enough? Personal is personal, even for pastors."

"It isn't enough," Elly said quietly. "Maybe it should be, but it isn't. People want to know, and they won't trust him until they do. You should ask Judah, Beck. He knows you aren't against him."

On the court, Judah was laughing and Jeremy was yelling at him to shut up and serve. How would Judah respond if I did ask him? Would he get angry? Lose confidence in our friendship? In me? Or would he know he could safely confide in me? Was it worth the risk?

Elly gave me time to think about it while the boys finished their match. She lay in the grass watching them, but I could not.

Jeremy shouted in triumph as he and Judah limped from the court and fell to the grass beside us. "Killed him again," Jeremy bragged.

"It was a good match, though," Elly said.

Smiling, I yanked on the bill of Judah's white baseball cap. "Feel like a walk?"

"Not really. Why?"

I swallowed. Hard. "I want to ask you something."

Elly bolted to her feet, lugged Jeremy to his, and dragged him away, babbling something about milkshakes.

Brilliant, I thought. Judah won't suspect a thing.

Judah sat up and smiled at me. A kind smile. An innocent smile. "Why do I feel conspired against?"

I could not look at him.

"What is it, Rebekah? Did I do something wrong?"

I shook my head. "Never mind, okay?"

His eyes remained on me. I knew that, even though I was staring down at the grass.

Slowly, he stood and stepped three or four feet away from me. "You want to know why Dad left his church." The realization had weakened his voice. "Like everyone else."

If only I could be innocent of the accusation. If only I could erase my conversation with Elly and my resulting willingness to risk hurting him the way I now knew I had. But I couldn't.

"Judah," I said, "your family is under so much pressure because people are wondering. If they knew, at least we'd be dealing with facts instead of hyperactive imagination."

Slowly, stiffly, he turned to face me, his eyes ablaze with emotion I had never seen in them. "It amazes me that none of you have thought to contact our assistant pastor in Alaska. I'm sure he'd fill you in."

I stood and went to him. "I'm sorry." I placed my hand firmly on his shoulder. "Judah, I'm sorry."

He pulled away, but not before I realized he was trembling. "Who's asking, Rebekah? You? Your sister? Your father?"

"Is it too late to retract the question?"

"Yes." He walked away from me, bent to pick up his tennis racket, and hurried toward the sidewalk.

I ran after him. "*I'm* asking. What could be so horrible that you can't tell *me?* If anyone has been a friend to your family here, it's me, and—"

"And now the game's over?" He glared at me until I lowered my eyes. "Time's up?"

"Judah, that's not fair."

"Nothing about this *is.*"

This time I let him walk away, unsure whether to be angry at him or disgusted with myself. Both, maybe. Or neither.

God, where are You in all this?

I felt like an ant crawling up a two-by-four in part of a house under construction. The house was going to be huge, I knew, but all I could see was the piece of wood in front of me, even though I knew that God was the Carpenter in charge. He must have a plan, but not being able to see past the end of my nose made me nervous.

As I sat there waiting for Jeremy and Elly, my uncertain anger forced me to admit that Judah's refusal to tell me frightened me. What could be so horrible? Really.

Unfortunately, my mind was all too eager to supply scenario after scenario in answer to that question. I cringed at each of them. Pastor Fenton would not allow a man to pastor anywhere with any kind of serious sin in his so-recent past. And furthermore, I was sure that Pastor Ewen possessed too much integrity to do anything like that anyway. But his silence was condemning him to all kinds of imagined guilt.

Judah was right. Nothing about this was fair.

"Rebekah?"

"Judah." I stood. Surprised, grateful that he'd come back, and a little scared. "I'm—"

He held up his hand. "*I'm* sorry. You don't deserve what I said . . . or felt. I know I *can* tell you, Rebekah. I've wanted to, I don't know how many times. You're not wrong to ask me, but . . ." He sat in the grass, leaning slightly forward as if his stomach hurt. "It's got to be Dad's decision . . . who and when. I have to respect that, even if I don't agree. Nothing that might happen could be any worse than what already is, but . . . he's . . . he's not thinking of himself."

I sat down beside him. "I think I understand."

"Friends?" he asked uncertainly, as if he expected me to say no.

"Always, Judah."

Chapter Nine

Rain poured in misty sheets from massive blue-black clouds, keeping Wednesday cold and tedious. The downpour was so heavy when we arrived at church for midweek service that Dad let us out by the doors before going to park the car.

I ran up the stairs and waited for him under the awning. Giving preference to the congregation, Pastor Ewen had designated the far corner of the lot for leadership parking. That was great on nice days, but by the time my father splashed up the steps to join me, water had penetrated his raincoat and beaded on his glasses. I grabbed his hand and hugged him. A wet teddy bear.

Judah met me in the entryway and had barely said hello when Michael Kramer stepped out of the hallway and slapped Judah on the back, smiling like an old college buddy.

"I heard your dad has been sick," he said.

Judah nodded, visibly suspicious of Michael's sudden concern. "He's fine tonight. Thanks."

"Are you sure?" Michael grinned. "We were looking forward to hearing you preach again. At least rude isn't boring."

Somewhere behind me, Tony Kramer laughed. Then he joined his big brother and the two of them strode into the sanctuary, congratulating each other.

"Just ignore them," I told Judah, reminded of two brats I had seen kicking their own puppy against the side of a garage. "Anyone with half a brain knows what they're trying to do."

"Which is?"

"Create tension."

He smiled. "It's working. If it keeps up too much longer, even brainless people are going to know what Michael looks like with a broken nose."

I laughed, but Mrs. Ewen did not share my delight at her son's thought. "I heard that," she said to him. "You hold your tongue and your temper. That's how you'll get through this right."

"I know."

Now she smiled. "I know you do." She walked with us to the sanctuary, where we sat together in the front row just as Pastor Ewen went to the pulpit.

At first I felt awkward, sitting with the Ewen family instead of with my own family. It had only happened because I thought we still had several minutes before the service. I would visit with them and then join my parents. But Pastor Ewen was already clipping the lapel microphone to his tie and asking us to bow our heads for prayer.

Too late to move now, I thought, not disappointed.

Amens having been exchanged, the pianist pounded out the chorus of a familiar hymn, which we proceeded to sing in its entirety—all eight verses and seven repetitions of the chorus. Pastor Ewen did not sing. He leaned against the back wall, his eyes closed.

"Is he all right?" I whispered to Rachel.

"Probably wants to save his voice for the sermon."

When the song ended, Pastor Ewen wiped his forehead with his handkerchief and stepped up to the podium. He squinted as he flipped through the thin pages of his Bible in search of his opening passage of Scripture. After directing us to Psalm 37, he began to read aloud. He missed a word in verse two and a line in verse four before stopping to apologize, rub his eyes, and begin again.

I leaned toward Rachel again. "He doesn't look good."

"He must have gotten a chill in the rain." Rachel glanced anxiously at her mother as Judah whispered something to Nathan. "He was fine when we left for church."

As Pastor Ewen attempted to reread the passage, his face flushed red and then, just as quickly, paled. He stopped, clutched the rim of the podium, and called for my father. "I'm sorry," he said, "I'm not well."

Mrs. Ewen rushed to him. Dad met her there—just in time to catch Pastor Ewen as he fell, unconscious, into him. Dad lowered him to the floor and quietly repeated his name while Mrs. Ewen knelt beside him to loosen his tie.

Rachel reached into her mother's purse, pulled out the key ring, and handed it to Judah. "Go bring the Jeep up," she told him.

He nodded and ran out of the church.

Dad and Mrs. Ewen spoke to Pastor Ewen. Several people from the congregation offered assistance. It seemed to happen so slowly, yet before I could think about what I should be doing to help, Dad, Judah, and Mr. Potts had carried Pastor Ewen outside, and Dad had returned and dismissed the service. He drove Elly and me home, then left to meet Mom and Mrs. Ewen at the emergency room.

By the next morning they still had not come home, and since I had spent the night watching shadows trek across my walls instead of sleeping—because I *could not,* I decided on my own to stay home from school. Dad would call and excuse me later.

But sitting in the kitchen in front of a bowl of soggy flakes was not what I needed.

I needed to know about Pastor Ewen.

As I stood at the sink rinsing my cereal bowl, I stared through the window at the street. Everything was still wet from yesterday's rain, but the sun was sparkling on the wet tips of the grass.

I would walk the two miles to the hospital.

The air and exercise would do me good. As would knowing, I hoped.

I dressed in warm, comfortable clothes and quickly brushed my hair, leaving it straight and down. I did not stop to tidy my room or make sure I had put the cereal back in the pantry. Nobody would care about those things today.

Before leaving, though, I did telephone the Ewen house.

No answer.

Since I did not know Pastor Ewen's condition or room number, I headed for the information counter when I arrived at the hospital.

"Can I help you?" The young man tending it spoke to me in a sickeningly kind voice.

"Yes. I . . . my pastor came in here last night, uh, Ben Ewen? I need to know what—"

"Rebekah."

I turned at the gentle tug on my sleeve. Mrs. Ewen nodded to the man at the counter, then led me toward a glass door at the far end of the lobby.

"I was going to the courtyard for air," she said as she pulled open the door. "Come sit with me."

"If you'd rather be alone . . ."

"Come with me."

Outside, I found my key ring in my jacket pocket and held it so tightly that my plastic *R* snapped. "How is he?"

"It isn't good."

"It *is* the flu, though, right?"

She nodded. "People do . . . die from it sometimes."

"They don't think . . . ?"

"They don't know yet."

Suddenly, the smug scent of lilac and the icy touch of fear squeezed around me so that I thought I wouldn't be able to breathe. I was grateful when we sat on a stone bench away from the lilacs. Water trickled into a small fountain behind us.

"I love springtime," Mrs. Ewen said.

"Me too."

"His temperature is real high. They haven't been able to touch it. His breathing is rough. He woke up this morning calling me Aunt Rose." Only now did Mrs. Ewen look at me, and she was smiling. "If you knew Ben's Aunt Rose, you would know why this disturbs me."

"I think Judah has mentioned her," I muttered, unable to return her smile.

"Has Judah also mentioned how his father and I met?"

"No."

"I suppose that wouldn't interest you."

She had tossed the bait, and the tease in her grin made me jump at it. "Yes it would."

She smiled. "I had always planned to be a missionary. When I started seriously considering *where,* my two older brothers, concerned for my future well-being, took it upon themselves to train me in the art of self-defense—although their version was more like a Saturday morning cartoon. After a few lessons, it was time for my first test. I was to stroll down this out-of-the-way street at dusk, and they were going to ambush me to test my instinct. Silly, really, but I agreed."

She laughed. "So, I'm walking, laughing to myself about how I was going to show them who was ready to go anywhere for Jesus, when there they were. I screamed and froze. They started shoving me around a bit, telling me what I should be doing. Well, out of this meat market across the street charged Ben and his younger brother, Connor, who I didn't know, of course. Before I could say anything, they had pinned my brothers against the wall, and Ben was asking me if I was okay. Why we had decided to do this exercise in public, I'll never know." She paused. "God knew, though."

"What did you do?" I asked, squirming at the thought of myself in that position.

"I told him that the thugs were my brothers."

"What did *he* do?"

She smiled up at the sun. "He looked at me as if I'd sprouted a second head, and released my brothers. He introduced himself and Connor, told us they were in D.C.—that's where I grew up—with their father for some kind of agricultural convention, and invited us out for ice cream. That was it."

"*It?* You knew right then? In the middle of the street?"

She shook her head. "I didn't see or hear from him again until two years later, when we just so happened—if you believe in coincidences—to end up on the same mission team in South America. His team.

"He looked exactly like in D.C., only older, and more captivating because of his position and his incredible knowledge of the Bible. He was amazing. Irritating, at times, but we couldn't help but respect him."

"Did he remember you?"

She nodded, shutting her eyes to enjoy the memory.

It was one of those moments again, when I should say something. But what? She had to be weary of hearing that God is in charge, or that Pastor Ewen was strong and would pull through this. What could I say that could really make a difference? Nothing. So we stared at the flowers and listened to the fountain.

"The hardest thing," she said after several silent minutes, "is being so completely helpless. I can't do a thing for Ben. I've always been able to fix things. A bloodied knee. A broken toy. A beaten ego. It's easy to say I trust God when I really don't have to. When I know that I can fix it with my own hands or the right words if God doesn't do the miracle. But my hands and words are useless now."

"Not your words to God," I said.

She smiled nervously, as if she thought she may have said too much, wiped her eyes, and hugged me. "You're right, Rebekah."

I wondered.

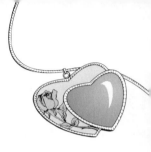

Chapter Ten

By Saturday morning, when Pastor Ewen's fever still hadn't responded consistently to medication or any other efforts to cool him, Rachel, Nathan, and Judah were fatigued, irritable, and in obvious need of a respite from hospital hallways. They refused to leave, though, complaining that the house was too quiet, too empty, and too far away from their father. Too unsettling.

So we stayed at the hospital until lunchtime, sitting beside Pastor Ewen two at a time. When Rachel and I had been in his room for an hour, and his only movement had been the unsteady rising and falling of his chest as he labored to breathe, I said, "Rachel, why don't we do something this afternoon? There's a carnival at the mall." Seeing reluctance in her eyes as she looked down at her father, I spoke again quickly. "We wouldn't be gone long. An hour or two." I smiled. "Trust me. If he knew how grumpy you guys are, he'd be the one asking you to leave for a while."

A strained smile touched her face as she held a cool cloth to her father's cheek. He stirred, but did not open his eyes. "Okay," she said. "An hour or two."

Nathan required more convincing, and Judah seemed to agree only out of duty to my thoughtfulness, but they all left the hospital with me.

That was the tough part, I thought. I can handle their moods.

We decided to stop at their house first. Rachel wanted to change clothes, and they all needed to pick up some money. Judah drove us in his father's Jeep, and the cassette of hymns already plugged into the tape deck spared us from sitting in silence.

"Give me five minutes," Rachel said, running upstairs to her room.

"You got it." Nathan sat beside me on the couch. "Will five dollars be enough? That's all I have."

Judah said, without looking at Nathan, "I have more if you need it." He replaced the picture of his parents' wedding that he had picked up from the telephone table near the stairs.

Beside me, Nathan stiffened. "I don't need anything from you."

In front of me, Judah flinched. I felt pressed—fearful of the unexplained emotion between him and Nathan, and trapped by it.

"I. . . I was only trying to help."

"What?" Nathan chuckled his contempt. "You think giving me two dollars to ride a roller coaster is going to make up for—"

"No, Nathan. I—"

"You *what?*" Getting to his feet like a man suddenly realizing his freedom, Nathan strutted across the room and stood right behind Judah. "What?"

Okay, I thought. Mood number one. I stood to handle it. "Guys, let's—"

"Say it! *Say it!*"

"Nathan, come on. This is stupid." I stepped up beside him. "He was just offering to give you money if you need it. You're tired. You're scared. That's okay, but don't take it out on—"

Nathan laughed. "There's another one protecting you, Judah. Another one telling me I'm wrong. Isn't that *nice.*" He spun Judah around to face him and shoved him against the wall. "But I'm not wrong. Am I?"

Judah stood paralyzed by the unbridled strength of Nathan's quiet fury. Nathan wasn't shouting. He was spitting. And Judah seemed powerless to oppose it.

Nathan's grip tightened around Judah's arms as he pressed in closer to him. "This is all because of you. All of it. No decent friend would have left Tommy the way you did. He wouldn't be dead, Judah. Dad wouldn't have lost his church. We wouldn't even be here. Dad would never have gotten this stupid flu, and he wouldn't be dying right now. If he does die, it's because of—"

"Stop it!" I grabbed a fistful of Nathan's red sweatshirt and yanked him away from Judah. My angry strength surprised us both. "Don't you dare say what you were about to say, Nathan. That's wrong. I don't care *what* happened in Alaska. That's wrong." I released my hold on him, unintentionally giving him a shove because I was shaking, then I ran to the bottom of the stairs. "Rachel," I yelled, "let's go!"

Nathan's unrepentant glare when I turned back toward him chilled me, but it was easier to handle than his words, although it said the same thing.

"I'll be outside," he said as he left, slamming the big front door.

Judah. I had to force myself to look at him. What kind of woundedness would I see in his eyes? An accusation like that . . . from his *brother*.

He sat on the bottom step. Defeated. Exposed. Looking like he'd met an undisguised demon face to face, and had only escaped by chance. But when I moved to approach him, he held up his hand and shook his head. "I'm . . . sorry you had to hear that," he said.

Though I wanted to run to him and hold him until he believed me when I told him it wasn't his fault, I stayed still. I did not know the situation. It was not my place to take sides. Even if I thought I should, Judah had made it clear that he would not receive my comfort. And how could he?

Still, when he placed his hand on my arm several long seconds later to lead me toward the door, I did not pull away. "Judah," I said, "you know we're friends. No matter what."

He nodded.

"Count on it."

He nodded again, and squeezed my arm before letting it go to open the door.

When Rachel joined us in the Jeep a few minutes later, still braiding her wet hair, Judah drove us to the mall and parked near the carnival fun house. He separated from us immediately, saying, with a smile that I did not believe, that he would be sick if he even looked at a ride. Too much hospital food, and all. "I'll go play some games," he told Rachel when she protested. Maybe he figured that hitting things with baseballs, arrows, and pillow hammers would help.

And he declined my offer to accompany him.

So Nathan, Rachel, and I rode together on almost every ride in the place. Twice. I tried not to let my uneasiness about Nathan's comments to Judah affect my behavior toward him. I laughed with him, shared my popcorn with him, and rode with him on three of the scariest rides when Rachel preferred to sit them out. But it wasn't fun. Not the way a carnival should have been.

Had I really expected it to be?

Their father was dying.

"We'd better get back," Rachel said when Nathan and I stumbled from one of the gravity rides.

"I'll go find Judah," I said. "We'll meet you at the Jeep."

I walked past all the games and through two side-show tents before I spotted him, sitting alone on a curb, watching a woman paint stars and rainbows on children's faces.

He stood when he saw me. "I won this for you," he said, handing me a small porcelain clown. It wasn't a gaudy clown, but delicate. Its precisely painted features, white satin body, and tiny porcelain hands and feet reminded me of one of those children's books that aren't only for children. "I had to win eight times to get it," Judah said. "But I figure you're past the stuffed green worm or purple and orange bubble-blowing hippo stage."

"Thank you," I said, laughing. "Bubble-blowing hippo?"

He nodded and smiled.

"Is that a real smile, Judah Ewen? Or a 'be bold and be strong' one?"

"It's a real one," he said.

"Good."

I walked back to the Jeep with him, holding the porcelain clown close to me.

Chapter Eleven

It was the middle of the night. My head hadn't quit hurting since that last gravity ride, and I couldn't sleep.

Maybe Dad was still awake.

I walked quietly along the dark hallway toward the light in the den. "Dad?"

"Beck." Dad closed his Bible and rubbed his eyes. "Can't sleep either, eh?"

"No."

"Come sit down." He patted the couch and put his arm over my shoulders as I sat beside him, then he waited while I nestled against him until I was comfortable. "What's on your mind?"

"Dad . . ." I sighed, not sure where I should begin, or if I even wanted to.

He didn't press me, and for several minutes, neither of us spoke. I could hear the steady ticking of our mantel clock—*tick tick tick tick*—like a hyperactive metronome. I could feel the slower beating of Dad's heart. My head rose and fell with his relaxed breathing, and I nearly fell asleep.

"Beck? How do you feel about Judah, exactly?"

I woke up fast. My father was asking me about the boy I liked. Wasn't that supposed to be some sort of sacred ground where fathers and daughters feared to tread together? Not for me. This was *Dad.* The man who had walked me to school and into my classroom the first day of kindergarten. The man who had cleared an entire afternoon's calendar of counseling appointments—without being asked—to cheer me on at my fifth-grade band audition. The man who had treated me like an Olympic gold-medalist after my not-so-outstanding first swim meet. He loved me, and I knew it. He desired good for me, and he demonstrated it. I could talk to him. Even about the boy I liked.

"It's kind of like a regular crush," I said. "I think he's attractive. I like his voice, and the way he says the things he says. But, it's more than that too."

"In what way?"

"That's the hard part." I flicked one of his nightshirt's oversized buttons with my fingernail. "It's like God meant us to be friends, or something. I know that sounds stupid and typical, but it's true. We just got along, right from the start, and without all that cutesy junk between us. It's honest."

"Would you date him? If he were allowed, and asked you?"

"Absolutely." I frowned. "Why are you asking me all this, Dad?"

He leaned his head against the back of the couch. "You need to be careful."

"Of?" I could feel a lecture coming on like a bad case of hay fever.

"He's been hurt, Beck. Badly hurt."

"I know."

"No. Listen to me. Esther told me today what happened in Alaska. She thought you might run into it, with her kids being as tired and edgy as they are. She wanted me to be prepared." He looked at me. "Was she right?"

I told him what Nathan had said to Judah. Everything. And I told him how I had responded.

He closed his eyes and exhaled through tight lips.

"Did I do wrong, Dad?" I sat up to see him clearly. "I didn't know what to do. Dad, if you had seen Judah's face . . ."

"You handled it right, Beck." He pulled me close again. "What I'm telling you stays here."

It wasn't a question, and we both knew it, but I gave him my word anyway.

"Judah and Tom Cook were best friends. Every summer for the past couple of years, they'd borrowed a couple of horses and gone camping. A dirt trail went up into a canyon and crossed a river on a plank-board bridge. There was a shortcut, though, through the woods and across the river at a shallow spot. This year, the river was high and fast, and full of debris from flooding upstream, so Ben asked the boys not to go off the trail at all. Judah can't swim, and Ben was concerned about the horses spooking in the quick water. The boys agreed and left."

He paused. "The rest of this is Judah's account of what happened—which is all anyone has. They rode up on the trail, camped, and had fun. But on the way back, Tommy decided he wanted to take the shortcut because it was going to rain. Judah says he argued with him, tried to talk him out of it, but finally said, 'You do what you want. I'm staying on the trail.' So Judah stayed on the trail, and Tommy took the shortcut." Dad's arm tightened around me. "Esther said that Judah was thinking Tommy would get scared about crossing alone and change his mind."

"But he didn't," I said.

"And he drowned."

I pushed myself free of Dad's hold and stood up. "That's not Judah's fault. How can they—?"

"Mr. Cook figured that Judah should have gone with Tommy because of the danger involved. You know, maybe he could have helped him."

"And maybe they both would have drowned." Sitting beside Dad again, my stomach felt as if someone was stomping on it. "Dad, that's not fair."

"That's Ben and Esther's opinion, but not Mr. Cook's."

"It's not a matter of opinion, Dad. The man—"

"The man lost his son."

I leaned forward, pushing my hair back with my hands and clutching it.

Dad gently rubbed my back. "Judah was asked to leave Tom's funeral. Ben—"

"That's cr—"

"Ben told Mr. Cook—his assistant pastor, remember—that if Judah couldn't stay, none of their family would. That suited Mr. Cook, so they all left."

"Oh, Dad."

"Ben and Mr. Cook couldn't resolve it, and soon the whole church was picking sides."

I leaned against Dad again, wanting to cry, but too angry.

"Judah took a lot of grief during that time," Dad said quietly. "Esther says he took it hard."

"Well, no doubt, Dad."

"After a couple of months, Ben saw that it wasn't doing his church any good—his hanging in there trying to work it out. And he had to get his son out of that. So he resigned, asked Pastor Fenton for a few months to work things through with his family, and went to Montana.

"Pastor Fenton supports Ben in this. He asked another pastor to take Ben's church in Alaska—someone he considered able to work Mr. Cook through his grief and put that church in order again. And after a few months, he sent Ben here."

I closed my eyes, trying to ignore the memory of the pain in Judah's eyes that afternoon. Now that I understood the full impact of Nathan's words, the memory felt like a wound of its own. How could Nathan do that to his brother?

I asked Dad.

"Nathan loved Tom too, Beck," Dad said. "He couldn't go to his funeral. . . . He's hurt. Like Judah. He just handles it differently. Esther says they've worked and worked with him. She doesn't think he actually blames Judah for Tom's death, but he needs someone to take it out on when the pressure's on."

I nodded. "But . . . doesn't he realize what he's doing to Judah?"

"Judah knows how Nathan really feels."

I had to disagree. "You didn't see his face, Dad."

"That's because Judah believes it. Nathan can't say anything Judah doesn't already think for himself. That's the problem, Beck, and that's where you need to be careful."

He twisted my hair. "He's vulnerable there. Too vulnerable. Like an Old Testament city with an unfinished wall. Anyone could march in the tiniest opening if the guard was down and destroy the entire city."

I understood. "Like a knight with a gash in his armor."

"Exactly." Dad shook a bit as he chuckled. "That's the romantic way of putting it." He grew still again. "But there's nothing romantic about it."

"I'll be careful," I said. "Should I tell him I—?"

The telephone rang.

We both jumped, then laughed.

"How long have you been in the ministry, Dad? You would think a late-night call wouldn't scare us anymore."

"They scare me," he said. "They're never good news."

"Maybe . . . Sara Dunn had her baby?"

"Even that wouldn't be good news." He lifted his arm above my head and grunted as he hefted himself out of his sink-hole in the couch. "It's six weeks early."

He answered the phone, listened quietly, turned away from me, said he would be there as soon as he could, and hung up. "That was your mother," he said, not looking at me.

"Dad?" I stood and went to him. Mom was at the hospital. She had spent every night there with Mrs. Ewen. She had not called home before. "Pastor Ewen . . . ?"

"No, Beck, but—"

I stopped hearing him there.

He wasn't dead yet, BUT . . . How could someone die of the flu, anyway? In a hospital? They can revive people whose hearts have stopped, who have been crushed by trains, whose kidneys have failed. How could someone die of the stupid flu in a hospital?

How, God?

I wanted to believe that God's purpose was being accomplished in all this. That He really was in control. At work in the situation, like His Word promises He will be.

But I couldn't see it. Not at this moment. And reminding myself about Joseph in Egypt—the way God used events that had been intended for evil to bring glory to Himself, provision for His people, and blessing to Joseph—wasn't helping very much.

"I'm going with you," I said, willing myself to stand straight and not cry. "Okay?"

"No."

"Dad, please." I did not whine like a child demanding new roller skates. I did not beg like a teenager desperate to borrow the car. I implored him with everything in me that mattered. "Please."

"No." He embraced me quickly, tightly, then hurried into the hallway. "The best thing you can do is stay here and pray."

I followed him. "How can I sit here and pray when Pastor Ewen is dying?"

Even in the hallway's dimness, I could see my father's shoulders yield to the weight of the imminent death of someone who had become his friend, and his daughter's misplaced desire to be there. He looked straight at me. "How can you not?"

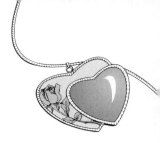

Chapter Twelve

At 9:15, the Kramers arrived at our house, shattering the Sunday morning stillness with three repugnant blasts of their green bomb's horn.

Just what I needed first thing in the morning. Especially this morning.

That horn. That car.

Those people.

Dad had not called. I had no idea whether Pastor Ewen had survived the night or not. Dad had taken the time to arrange a ride to church for Elly and me; why couldn't he have found one moment more to call home?

Didn't he know I had not slept?

I had prayed, like he'd said. And then I'd prayed that God's answer to my prayer would be *yes*. And then I had sat in the dark. Waiting.

"Good morning, Rebekah," Mr. Kramer said to me when I sat in the back seat of his car beside Michael.

"Morning," I muttered. He'd gotten my name right, and that scared me.

"Your father said to tell you about Ben . . ."

My stomach tightened while he waited for Elly to get in and shut the door.

"His fever broke sometime this morning," he said. "The doctor thought it was going to go the other way."

"He's going to be okay?" Elly asked, with the same hopeful *Please say yes* in her voice that was holding my breath.

"It's too early to say for sure," he said, "but it looks that way."

Yes! Thank God! Yes!

I said, "Whew. That's good."

"Yes, it is," Mr. Kramer said.

Mrs. Kramer agreed. "A lot of people were praying."

Prayer.

Was that the reason Pastor Ewen was well now, or did he just . . . recover? Was it luck or coincidence, or miracle? Natural, or divine? The question was not a new one, and its answer would probably not be proven here on earth, but I knew what I believed about it.

And if he had died? What would you believe then?

An army of questions surrounded my fort of faith, but I sent them retreating with three words: *God is sovereign.*

Either way, God is sovereign.

Of course, this assurance came easily now because God had chosen to show His sovereignty in the way that I had prayed He would. I could only hope that I would be as confident even if He had not.

This time, though, He had, and all I wanted to do was thank Him. So I did.

Pastor Ewen was released from the hospital Monday afternoon. He spent all day Tuesday with his family and most of Wednesday with my father and Mr. Kramer.

"He's going to call a special board meeting after service tonight," Dad told me as he helped me clear the dinner dishes from the table. "He's decided to tell them about Tom Cook."

"Why?"

"He thinks it's time."

"Does Judah know?"

Dad nodded. "He's been pressing Ben to do it all along."

Of course he has, I thought.

Knowing that protecting *him* was costing his father the confidence of his board probably troubled Judah more than any conceivable reaction to the truth, but . . .

I nearly slammed my hand in the refrigerator putting away the leftover meat loaf. The board seemed too eager to find fault, oppose, and believe evil about Pastor Ewen. Could they be trusted to see beyond the potential in Tom Cook's death to get at this new pastor? Surely they would assent to Judah's innocence regarding it, but mightn't they use it against his father anyway?

"Beck, most of the men have kids," Dad said, placing his hand over mine as if he had read my mind. "They'll handle it right. I'm confident of that." He smiled. "They still may not like Ben, but this won't be part of it."

"What if you're wrong?"

"Then we'll handle it."

I needed more than that.

I needed a sense of their reaction to the information. Of what we could expect, and from whom.

I needed to find out more about this board meeting than my parents would ever confide in me.

Right or wrong, I knew of a way to do that.

After the service, I left the other kids in the entryway and slipped, unnoticed, into the ladies' restroom. I locked the door, stared in the mirror for several seconds, wrestling with what I was about to do, then crouched on the floor beside the open heat vent—the one that opened on the other side into the board room.

Pastor Ewen wasted no time.

"Thank you all for coming on short notice," he began. "I want to address something that's going on here a bit more seriously than I realized. If we, as leadership, are going to accomplish God's purpose for us in this church, we need to trust each other so that we can work as a team. I've been leery of trusting you, and you've been unable to trust me. We need to correct that. I'm here to start us going in that direction. Esther?"

Papers rustled, and men muttered thanks.

"These are copies of a letter I wrote to Pastor Fenton, explaining the circumstances of my resignation. I think it includes all the information you'll need."

Nobody spoke. I assumed that they were reading.

"I'm sure it's plain to you that giving out this information puts my son at significant risk—which is why I had hoped to avoid doing it. I must ask you to please keep this in confidence. He has gone through enough over this thing. I won't let him go through any more."

"Are you threatening us, Ben?"

"You can easily see why this is important, Mr. Cox."

Dad asked if he could speak.

"As church leaders," he said, "we know that our personal lives will often come under excessive scrutiny. At the same time, we all need—and have a right to—a certain amount of privacy. Please respect this need for Ben and Judah as much as you would want us to respect it for you or your child."

"Thanks, Rick," Pastor Ewen said.

"Listen," someone said. I wasn't sure I recognized his voice. "It's obvious, if this account is accurate, that Judah wasn't responsible for this boy's death."

"It's accurate," Mrs. Ewen blurted.

The man continued with a slight hint of impatience in his tone. "I can understand your reluctance to share this with us, Ben, what with church politics being the way they sometimes are. But we're all reasonable men. We can see that you are trusting us with something personal and dangerous if mishandled. We'll respect that . . . at least, *I* will."

"Thank you, Mr. Potts."

Some men mumbled agreement, but not ten. I hoped the others were nodding theirs.

"If I can," Pastor Ewen said, "I'd like to clear up one other thing. That remark Judah made to Mr. Cox all those weeks ago? He did make a mistake. He knows it. He repented. Let it rest."

Someone coughed.

"That kid sure causes you a lot of trouble."

A silence, and then, "Mr. Dunn, your son isn't born yet. When he is, you'll discover that there's something about leadership kids—particularly pastors' kids—that inspires a little more watching from people, and a lot more judgment. My kids are just that . . . kids. Just like any other kids. They're young. They make mistakes. They aren't above correction, but what has been going on with Judah is not correction. I can understand other kids clinging to his indiscretion and harassing him about it, but we are adults. Some of you must either think we're deaf or want us to hear what you're saying behind our backs. If you have a problem with my kids or with me, bring it to me outright. I'm not the kind of man who has to be gotten at by beating around the bush. I am willing to hear and act on your concerns. You needn't feel I can't or won't work with you here. We have got to trust each other and be united as leadership if—"

"You don't seem too good at procuring that, Mr. Ewen."

"That's for sure," an old voice agreed. "It seems to me that if that was truly your goal, you would have let the kid take the heat. You know, stick it out and let God show who was right in the end. Maybe your church would have stayed behind you then."

"Mr. Talbot, we're talking about the 'heat' of being responsible for someone's death." For the first time, anger tensed Pastor Ewen's voice. "Which of you would put that kind of burden on an innocent kid—*your* kid—to save your own position?"

That shut them up.

"I'm willing to do what it takes to make this work," Pastor Ewen said wearily after a few moments of silence. "God put us together here for a reason. I don't want us to miss, or prolong it, or to think to ourselves that He must have gotten it wrong this time." He chuckled. "Life would've been a whole lot easier on Jonah if he had just gone to Nineveh the first time. God's will still got done, just like it will here because God is God. The question is, do we need to do some time in the fish's belly first? I hope not." He paused. "I know some of you have problems with me. Let me hear them. Right now if you like."

Nobody spoke.

"Okay," Pastor Ewen said slowly. "Let's, uh, close in prayer, then. Joe, would you pray, please?"

Someone turned the bathroom doorknob.

I bolted to my feet, called, "Just a minute," and went to the sink to wash my hands. I felt as though they couldn't get clean enough. Fortunately, the girl I let in when I left was only seven years old. She would not notice how clearly one could hear through the open heat vent.

Just ahead of the people coming out of the board room, I made a point to display my happiness about rejoining the Ewen kids in the entryway, and I yearned aloud for an ice-cream sundae.

Judah smiled. "That does sound good."

"Why not do it, then?" Pastor Ewen approached us and placed his hand squarely on Judah's shoulder. "Rick?"

"Anytime," Dad said.

Pastor Ewen invited everyone. Half accepted his invitation. Half declined. It was as if a trumpet had sounded in our little portion of Zion, and the armies were choosing up sides.

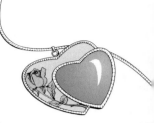

Chapter Thirteen

To my surprise and delight, the last week and a half of school passed quickly, exams and all. When I returned home and tossed my book bag into the hall closet for its summer hibernation, I raised my right hand and shouted praises.

One year of high school to go! The best year.

The aroma of barbecued chicken lured me to the patio. I grabbed a serving fork from the pile of silverware on the picnic table and smiled at Mom. "Are you starved, pregnant, or what?"

"Very funny. We're having company."

"Who?"

"The Ewens." She smiled at my smile. "Your father and Ben have some serious talking to do about the thing with Mr. Cox."

"What thing?"

Mom grimaced—that *Oops, I slipped* kind of look. Then she sighed and said, "Oh, Beck, you're going to find out sooner or later, anyway. Mr. Cox was in a car accident yesterday."

"Oh, no. Was he hurt?"

"No. The woman in the other car was, though. Not seriously, thank God, but she was."

"How'd it happen?" I asked, although I suspected I already knew. Mr. Cox's eyes had been growing worse and worse lately, but he was too independent to admit it.

"Beck, he turned a corner and drove right into her." She frowned. "He didn't see her."

"Well, at least nobody was seriously hurt," I said. "And maybe some good will come out of it. Maybe he'll reconsider Dad's suggestion to find someone to drive for him."

"That's part of the problem, Beck. He should have done that last fall when his license wasn't renewed because of his eyesight."

So, he had been driving illegally. "What are Dad and Pastor Ewen going to talk about?"

"Ben asked Mr. Cox to resign his position on the board."

"What?" I hadn't expected that. "Why? Everyone's okay. It wasn't like he was drunk or anything."

Mom nodded. "But a church leader 'must be blameless' and 'have a good report of them which are without; lest he fall into reproach and the snare of the devil.' "

"What does that mean, exactly?"

Mom smiled. "It means that Ben doesn't want his board members doing illegal things."

"Well, when you put it like that," I said. Still, I had to think about it. "Isn't asking him to resign a little extreme, though? I mean, everyone loves Mr. Cox. He's been at the church forever."

Mom shrugged. She was still thinking about it, too. "It's the old Grace vs. Law dilemma. Every pastor leans a little differently."

My fork slipped and a chicken wing fell into the coals. It turned black before I could jab it and pull it out. "This isn't going to win any points with the rest of the board for Pastor Ewen," I said. "But he's right . . . I guess. I mean, blameless and illegal don't exactly go together."

"No, they don't," Mom agreed.

"Still, it seems a little harsh."

"That's because we love Mr. Cox."

That was true. If some stranger had done what Mr. Cox had, I'd probably get angry and say something like "Get over your pride and take a cab before you kill someone." But Mr. Cox . . . his humorous pride was one of the things that endeared him to us. "And 'love covers a multitude of sins,' " I muttered.

"But the law doesn't," Mom pointed out.

A dog barked on the other side of our back fence.

"What does Dad think?" I asked Mom.

"He agrees with Ben," she said. "And, believe it or not, so does Mr. Kramer, though neither of them likes it much."

"The other board members?"

Mom began piling chicken pieces onto a platter. "About half and half," she replied. "But the ones who are upset are *really* upset."

Poor Pastor Ewen, I thought. If it isn't one thing, it's everything else.

When the Ewens arrived, Elly escorted them out to the patio. After Dad and I carried out the remaining food and placed it on the table, we all clasped hands while Nathan prayed, then we served ourselves buffet style and sat wherever we could find a place. I sat in the grass near the back fence. When Judah sat beside me, I felt embarrassed because he had taken significantly less food than I had.

"What do you do all day during summer?" he asked me.

"Laze around," I said with a smile. "Why?"

"I hate having nothing to do."

"That's because you think too much."

He chuckled and shooed a fly from his potato salad. "I know. But I don't know how not to. I mean, do you think about blackness, or what?"

Laughing, I said, "I couldn't tell you. I have the opposite problem."

"You know what they say about opposites." He pointed a carrot stick at me. "Have you ever wondered who those all-knowing 'they' are?"

"Not recently, no."

"They sure talk a lot," he said.

"Just like someone else we all know and love." Iced tea spilled out of my glass when I laughed. "Will you please be quiet and eat before someone chokes?"

He stayed quiet long enough for me to enjoy two bites of corn on the cob. Then he said, "I wonder who the first person was to try eating a potato."

This time, iced tea sprayed out of my mouth. "Judah, who cares?"

He was laughing. "Well, I mean, would *you* eat one if you just saw it lying around and didn't know it was food?"

"I guess not." Why was he talking so profusely about nothing? Judah had never been shy or quiet, but he usually trimmed his speech of everything unimportant.

"And chips." He held a potato chip out toward the sun and contemplated it. "Who thought to slice and fry them—or whatever they do to make them?"

When he returned his chip to his plate, I noticed that he'd only been pushing his food around. He hadn't eaten anything. I picked his chip back up and shoved it into his mouth. "Someone who wanted us to eat them," I said. "Not study them."

He swallowed it. Hard. "Isn't Dewey Mall near here?"

"Five blocks," I said.

"Maybe we could all walk over there when we finish. Give our parents time to hash things through."

"Good idea."

Nathan, Elly, and Rachel agreed, so we walked the five blocks as a noisy group and split up at the mall according to shopping interests.

Elly and Rachel disappeared behind a coat rack in a trendy clothing store. "Do you want to come to the bookstore with me?" Judah asked Nathan and me.

"No way," Nathan said, smiling. "I'm going to go look at computers."

Judah looked at me.

"The bookstore?" I asked

He nodded. "I'm sorry. I like to read."

"Don't be sorry."

I went with him. For the company, not the shopping. Bookstores, and especially their history sections—which Judah headed straight toward, bored me. As he slid books from the shelves and skimmed their introductions, I scanned titles. Of all the ways authors had managed to say "Civil War" without actually saying it, none of them intrigued me.

"This one looks good," Judah said.

How could he tell? The book was a thick volume with only words on its cover. Plain gray words.

I leaned against the edge of the shelf and glanced down the aisle toward the store entrance. I thought I had heard Michael Kramer's obnoxious laugh, and unfortunately, I was right. "Michael and Tony are here," I told Judah.

He stiffened. "Yeah?"

"They're over in the horror fiction section." I giggled. "How appropriate."

Michael saw me. I knew because his face oozed into that stupid grin of his. He snatched a book from the shelf, tapped Tony's arm, and strutted toward me.

"Hey, Cahill," he said. "I found a book your friend should read."

"Which friend, Michael?"

Judah stepped in beside me then and greeted Michael and Tony.

Michael grinned again. "Hmm. I've got the perfect book for you, Ewen." He held up the book he had been holding behind his back, displaying its gruesome cover. A seaweed-draped human form with blood dripping from one of its three fangs stood knee-deep in murky water. The book's title, *The Deep Cries Vengeance,* was done in the color of sewer sludge. Michael lowered the book and smiled. "It's about this kid who drowns and comes back, a living but dead monster, to eat his friend who didn't save him."

"I don't read that junk." Judah grabbed his Civil War book and pushed past Michael and Tony.

Michael followed him. "It's really suspenseful. The kid chases his friend everywhere. Sure you don't want it? I'll buy it for you."

"Save your money, thanks."

Judah endured the long line in spite of Michael's grotesque comments, and even put together a smile for the clerk when he paid her.

Michael knew . . . and obviously thought I didn't.

Judah thanked the clerk, tucked his sack under his arm, nodded at Tony and Michael, and led me out of the store. Quickly out. When we had walked past three other stores, he asked me, "Where to, now? Rachel wants a leather coat. I figured for graduation I—"

"Judah . . ." After making sure that Michael had not followed us, I touched his arm and waited for him to look directly at me. He seemed reluctant. "Judah, I know about Tommy. I know what happened. Your mom told my father the day we—"

"She told me that," he said. "But I didn't know he'd told you."

"I didn't know how to bring it up," I confessed. "I knew you wanted to tell me yourself."

He nodded.

"What are you going to do about Michael?"

"Nothing."

"Nothing? Judah, you've got to tell your father. He made it clear he wouldn't tolerate any—"

Fierceness in his eyes shut my mouth. "I don't have to tell him, Rebekah. He's got enough going on now with Mr. Cox."

"It won't stop if you don't stop it now." I tried to penetrate the hardness in his eyes with softness in mine. "You've got to tell your father. Mr. Kramer must have told—"

"I'm not going to tell him." There was no give in his blue-gray eyes. "And neither are you."

"What if Michael keeps after you?"

"I can take it."

I released his arm, appalled that he would stoop to the tough-guy thing. "Did I say you couldn't?"

"I only meant that—"

"I know exactly what you meant." I straightened my back, flexed my arm muscles, and grunted in a deep sluggish voice, "Me man. Me stand alone against everything."

He laughed. "Not exactly. I just figure I can put up with a little grief to save Dad some. He's certainly done more than his share of that for me."

I felt like the bottom of a rancher's boot on a rainy day. "I'm sorry."

"No problem."

But I knew there was still a problem. A big problem.

"It isn't as though I hadn't expected this," he said.

"It shouldn't be like this." We started walking again, heading toward one of the mall's three department stores. "There is going to be a day when this is over," I told him. "Behind you. Finished."

He smiled. "Will you put up with me in the meantime?"

"Well," I said with a laugh, "only if you buy me an ice-cream cone."

"I'll buy you two," he said, "in case it takes a while."

Chapter Fourteen

Allison Chaney ran toward me, dragging her denim tote bag. We hugged, pulled apart to look at each other, and embraced again. Travellers with planes or people to catch hurried past us.

"A year is too long," she said. "Look at you. You're gorgeous."

"Only half as gorgeous as you." As usual, Allison embodied *chic*. Her brown hair was strikingly short. Her face had been skillfully painted. Her clothes and physique were as suspiciously sensible as ever. "How's New York?" I asked her. "Your dad?"

"Busy." She shrugged. "You know. But it's okay. I'm meeting lots of new friends."

"Like Derik?" I giggled and elbowed her as we walked toward the baggage claim area.

"My usual dreamboat." She flipped her wrist and let her hand hang limp at her side. "Tall. Blond. Blue eyes. Football team. Blah blah blah. Jerk."

"Jerk?"

"Jerk. But hey, it's okay. I'm still young and gorgeous, and there are plenty of guys in the world. Speaking of guys, how's . . . uh . . . Josh, is it?"

Same old Allison. "Judah. It's Judah."

"Unique name. But, hey, unique is good. So how is he?"

"Fine."

"Fine?" She tilted her head so that her earrings jingled. "I'm not asking for a medical report, Becky. How is he in relation to you?"

"We're friends."

"*Friends* is an ambiguous term." She grinned. "Definition, please."

I laughed. "Don't ask for the wedding date yet, Allison. We're not dating. We're good friends."

"He likes someone else?"

"No." My defensiveness and the sting of the suggestion surprised me. "His dad is strict about dating. He can't until he's eighteen."

"How old is he now?"

"Just turned seventeen."

"Well, isn't there someone you could date until he turns eighteen?" She was serious.

I tried not to reveal too much of my annoyance at her comment. "Allison . . . no."

"Whatever," she said.

As we collected her bags, walked out to the car, and drove home, Allison kept talking, but an unfamiliar awkwardness hung between us. It made me wonder what had changed. Or who.

"So, when do I get to meet this guy? Judah."

"Tonight if—"

"Do you still see Jeremy?"

I nodded. "In fact, he and Judah—"

"Is that *him?*" she squealed as I pulled the car into our driveway. She pointed a long red fingernail at Jeremy's red pickup.

"That's him." I smiled. "And Judah."

I stepped out of the car and walked toward Judah.

Allison jumped out of the car and slammed into Jeremy's arms before he could even close his pickup door. He stood there with Allison clinging to him, patting her shoulder nervously.

"I hope I can assume they know each other," Judah whispered to me, grinning.

"They dated last year. Didn't Jeremy tell you?"

"No."

Ugly memories pursed my lips. "Yeah. That breakup was hard on him."

"Well, it doesn't look like it was too hard on her."

"It was," I said. "That's just Allison. Hey, it's okay. Pick up and move on."

Judah nodded.

When she finally unhanded Jeremy, Allison announced that she was famished and started to suggest pizza, but seeing Judah sidetracked her. She approached him, swinging her long-strapped black purse. "So, you're Judah." Appraising him without the slightest effort to hide it, she smiled and cleared her throat four times—each *ahem* representing a notch on her Gorgeosity Scale on which five *ahem*s marked the epitome. "Pastor's son. Can't date till you're eighteen and don't mind ruining Becky's social life in the meantime even though you obviously adore her. Play tennis with Jeremy. Anything else I should know about you as my best friend's . . . good friend?"

Judah laughed. "That's all the important stuff."

His laughter did not fool me. His eyes had gone serious with that familiar compassion of his. Allison's lostness had impacted him. Mood and conversation were trivial now, so he had laughed, but I had no doubt that he would stay alert for an opportunity to share with her what was truly most important—his faith.

For now, though, pizza.

Allison selected the place and then our booth once we got there. After that she immediately requisitioned Jeremy for one of their ritual video game challenges.

At the table beside ours, a young boy's birthday celebration was in noisy progress. Two frenzied women. Twelve preschoolers. Pizza. Presents. Noisemakers. Baby sister. *Have a nice lunch, ladies.*

"Look who's here, Tony."

Startled, I redirected my attention to the other side of our table. Michael and Tony Kramer were standing there. I looked at the preschoolers again, hoping that Tony and Michael would get the hint and go away, but they didn't.

"Does Daddy know that you're here alone with pretty Miss Rebekah?" Michael asked Judah, leaning over the table.

Judah smiled. "Hi, Michael. Tony. We aren't here alone."

"That's true," Tony said, nudging his brother.

"I guess it is," Michael said. "*We're* here with you." He slid into the bench across from us and yanked Tony down to sit beside him. Leaning forward, he tipped some grated Parmesan onto the table top, and then, one gritty grain at a time, started flicking it. "But your father doesn't know that, does he? I mean, you two could tell him whatever you think he wants to hear, and he's got only your word to go on."

Judah sighed, "I hear you fly remote-controlled helicopters."

"It's nice Paster Ewen trust his kids, don't you think, Tony?"

"Yeah. A regular nice family."

"Don't you two have friends to terrorize?" I asked, and received Judah's elbow in the ribs for it.

"What about you, Tony?" Judah asked. "What do you do for fun?"

Tony ate a handful of dried peppers. "I go fishing."

"There you go." Michael grinned. "That is a choice example of what I was just talking about. Let's take what happened to your friend . . ."

"No." Judah tensed beside me. "Let's not."

"Anything could have happened to him, right? I'm not saying you lied . . . I'm saying you *could* have. Your father trusts you, so he'd believe you. Convenient when you're the only one left to tell what happened."

"I didn't lie."

Under the table, my hand found Judah's and clasped it. The squeeze was returned and held.

"Nobody knows, though," Tony said. "Not for certain."

"You weren't invited to sit here," I reminded him, wishing for the nerve to spit. "Get lost."

"They can stay," Judah said, standing. "We'll go."

Michael stood with him. "Who knows? Maybe you two got in a fight over . . . your buddy's girl? . . . and things got out of hand and you—"

Judah steadied his face and looked directly at Michael. "I know what you're doing," he said evenly. "I have no intention of letting you succeed." He turned away. "Come on, Rebekah."

Neither Michael nor Tony said a word as Judah led me away from the table.

What were they thinking?

I allowed Judah to drag me within a few feet of Jeremy and Allison. "Judah," I said, stopping him, "promise you'll tell me when it's too much."

In his face, when he turned to look at me, I saw his determination, his fight, his pride. In his eyes I saw fear. Fear that the ghoulish monster of Michael's bookstore prank might someday catch and devour him. Not Tom Cook zombified, but his haunted and unresolved memory. Not draped in seaweed, but in the guilt, blame, and bitterness of others. This monster was being kept alive by Judah as much as by Michael, and *that* terrified *me*.

"I'll tell you," he said. "Don't worry, okay?"

But I did worry. More and more as summer pressed in on us with its hot days and quick fiery emotions.

Allison stayed ten days with me, during which we failed to share even one heartfelt conversation. Somewhere in the twelve months and twenty-two hundred miles that now separated us, and somehow, in the people we were becoming, she and I had surrendered something of our friendship. This intangible distance, which could not be regained with two weeks and a plane ticket every summer, disheartened me more than the physical separation. But I loved Allison, and saying good-bye again still hurt.

After she left, I could only pray that the things that Judah, Jeremy, and I did manage to tell her about Christ when she allowed us in beyond the trivial—which wasn't very often, would stay with her, and maybe, someday, help her.

Summer. Long, hot summer. I drifted sleepily through it. Eating drippy ice-cream cones. Swimming. Lying in prickly grass to admire the night skies. Retreating to air-conditioned malls. Reading fiction in the fat chair in the den, trying to convince myself that everything in real life would work out in the end, the way it always did in books.

But, my life wasn't a book. If it were, Pastor Ewen, bruised by opposition, but never broken, would perform some heroic deed—perhaps rescue Mr. Cox from his flaming car after he'd blindly driven full speed into the side of the church. The board, seeing Pastor Ewen's willingness to risk his own life for his adversary, with tears in their eyes and a new contract—including a sizable increase in his salary—in their hands, would beg Pastor Ewen to forgive them and stay on as pastor forever. Our church, humble though it may be, would march on to do irreproachable exploits for God because of our impenetrable unity of purpose.

Right.

Mr. Cox was not about to explode his car outside the church, but he certainly kept things hot and foul smelling *inside*. He enjoyed more power off the board than he had ever managed to accrue while serving on it. Bitterness in about half of the board members regarding his dismissal hovered like smoke over and around every decision the board tried to reach, blurring vision, tightening hearts, and permeating everything else.

Though Pastor Ewen's sermons, throughout July and early August, continued to provoke me toward the ideal of what it means to be a Christian, being so consistently overrun by reality fractured my confidence that the biblical ideal could truly be attained. But I kept hoping in Pastor Ewen's words because I believed that God would be faithful to complete whatever good work He had begun here, and because of Pastor Ewen's aggressiveness toward living what he preached, even in the midst of contention with those who should have been his support.

Judah, for his part, survived the summer in books. Always non-fiction. Always historical. Always about war. His moods had become increasingly unpredictable as a result of Michael's continued brutal teasing, but he refused to discuss any of it. If I asked, he ignored me. If I persisted, he rebuked me.

Whenever I thought he was being prideful about not admitting his need, foolish and stubborn in his refusal to go to his father, or insensitive to the fact that other people carried burdens too, I did not say it. Most often, I convinced myself that pride, foolishness, and insensitivity on *my* part were responsible for these feelings, and not him.

But his retreat into himself hurt me. It kept me at arm's length when I knew he needed me . . . as well as when I could have used support from him.

Still, he had become my closest, most treasured friend.

Until he forgot my birthday party.

"I'm sorry, Rebekah," he said, standing at my front door two hours after everyone else had gone home. The mid-August evening sun was beating into his back, but he was rubbing the sleeve of his sweatshirt as if he felt cold. "I . . . I forgot."

"You *forgot?*"

He nodded. "I'm sorry."

"Judah, you've known about it for weeks."

"I know." He shifted his weight. "I left early this morning for a bike ride and just . . . kept going. I forgot. The mountains were so peaceful and beautiful. I just forgot. I'm sorry."

"Yeah, well . . ."

Neither of us spoke for a long, unpleasant moment. Judah stood there, waiting for my understanding, and I stood there, refusing to give it to him. If he had been sick, or had lost his way, or had had one of his run-ins with Michael, then . . . maybe. But he had flat-out forgotten. That felt like a knife in the stomach, and he wasn't going to mend it that easily. Not this time.

"I brought your present," he said quietly, and held out a small, delicately wrapped box.

"Did Rachel wrap that for you, Judah?" I asked, allowing more of my anger into my tone than I had intended. But it fit. "Hey, maybe she even picked it out for you. Too bad she was working today. She could have reminded you to show up at the party, too."

"Rebekah, I—"

"I don't want your present."

The hurt in his eyes pulled at me to forgive him. It really wasn't that big a deal, was it? Yes. I looked past him, out into the empty street. He had hurt me, and for once, my need was going to be more important than his.

"Okay," he said finally, lowering his arm to his side again. "I'm sorry."

"Go home, Judah."

He opened his mouth to say something else, then changed his mind and turned, walking quickly to his bike. He unlocked it from my fence, jumped on it, and rode too fast around the corner.

I slammed the door shut and turned to run to my room so I could cry and smash the porcelain clown he'd given me against the wall.

He didn't care about me. He just needed a strong friend. And I, stupid, generous, and gullible, had allowed myself not to see it, and to excuse it when I did.

"Beck?"

I had run into Dad.

"I, uh, overheard you and Judah," he said. He held me while I first fumed and then sobbed. "Beck, is he okay? He didn't look—"

"Is *he* okay?" Every muscle in my body stiffened as I yanked myself away from Dad. "I don't believe you're asking me if *he* is okay. *He* forgot my party, Dad. He was too busy looking at . . . at *pine cones* to come to my birthday party. He's supposed to be my friend. My best friend. Why doesn't that matter? It's always him. Always. 'Is Judah okay?' Well, what about me? I'm not okay, Dad."

He smiled. "I guess I got told."

Hating to, because Dad could always make me do it, I laughed. "Yes, you did." I wiped my eyes.

"I'm sorry you're hurt, Beck."

"I don't want to talk about it, Dad. I know you think I'm being unreasonable about a stupid little thing. Someday, I'll probably agree. But right now I'm furious, and I don't want to talk about it." This usually worked with Dad. I hoped it would now.

"Okay." His hand dug deep in his pocket and found some coins to jingle. "But, I am concerned about Judah. He looked done in."

"He's been riding over rivers and through the woods all day, remember?"

"I don't mean that kind of done in."

I knew what Dad meant. I had noticed too but was willing myself not to care. Lifeless eyes, paleness, and an unwillingness to look directly at a person did not negate the fact that the boy had forgotten something that was important to his supposed best friend.

"Is everything okay between him and Nathan?" Dad asked.

"As far as I know," I replied flatly. I did not want to discuss Judah. Especially not *his* problems. But . . . something in me yearned, as I looked up at my father again, to tell him everything about Michael Kramer's teasing. That would put an end to Judah's most potent stress, but it would also lead to all-out war between Pastor Ewen and Mr. Kramer, and Judah would never forgive me for that.

Besides, I had given him my word.

He would handle it.

And, you don't care now anyway, remember?

Chapter Fifteen

After a frustrating night of half-sleep, I awoke fully to Elly's pounding on my bedroom door.

"Come on, Beck. The bus leaves in an hour."

"I'm up," I muttered.

For the first time since becoming a teenager, I was not elated by the prospect of leaving for youth camp. But I determined as I showered, ate breakfast, and finished my last-minute packing, not to let a grievance with someone who was not-even-my-boyfriend ruin a week I had been looking forward to all year.

When we arrived at the church parking lot, I hurried to hug my parents and board the coughing bus. Rachel was sitting about halfway back, beside Judah, glaring accusingly at me. I smiled at her and sat across the aisle beside Nathan.

He turned away to stare out the window.

Okay, I thought, biting my lip. He forgets my birthday and I'm the evil one. Just to prove how evil I could be, I did not move to find another seat.

These were my friends.

The bus jerked when its door hissed shut, and we were on our way to Wyoming. Unable to be at camp himself until later in the week, our youth pastor had chosen a driver who was more than competent to manage a busload of teens. He was a tall, thick prison guard by profession, and we gave him no reason to stop the bus.

The camp was staffed by counselors and aides who stayed at the lake all summer while each week brought in a new batch of kids from one or a few churches, depending on the size of their youth groups. Our youth group wasn't big enough to fill the camp, so we would be meeting new kids. Everyone was excited.

Including me.

But even though I liked all the girls in my cabin and enjoyed the camp activities and Bible lessons, the first two days were difficult and uncomfortable. Judah and I were ignoring each other—and working hard to do it. I no longer felt angry at him for forgetting my party, but I had to defend the Principle of the situation. I had to hold out for the apology due me. Not "I'm sorry I forgot your party," but, "I'm sorry I considered your emotions unimportant in comparison to my own." But this holding out was costing me. My entire body rallied against it. My heart kept reminding me of the concept of forgiveness. My stomach informed me in churning unpleasant ways that it would prefer a quick resolution, thank you very much. My appetite had vanished. I could not sleep. And my fingernails looked as if I had filed them in a pencil sharpener.

But I was going to hold out, even if it took all week.

To the great credit of our camp director, Pastor James, I had fun at camp in spite of Judah and the Principle. Pastor James was a powerful, no-nonsense speaker—a lot like Pastor Ewen—who conveyed ideas about things like purity, honesty, and keeping ourselves unstained by the world in such a way that we not only felt that we *should* do them, but *could, by the grace of God.* This concept encouraged me, and I tried to immerse myself in it.

Wednesday before evening chapel, I decided to spend free time alone. I wanted, and needed, to pray. For half an hour I walked through the trees along the lake, and then climbed a hill to sit in the shade and watch the other kids swim. Amazingly, because of the breeze in the branches above my head, I could hardly hear anyone, and the place relaxed me.

"Rebekah?"

I opened my eyes. Had I fallen asleep? I wasn't sure. "Judah." I squinted up at him and said nothing else.

"I saw you come up here," he said, sitting beside me. "Rebekah, I . . . I'm sorry."

It was the first time I had seen him face to face since arriving at camp. He looked like he hadn't slept at all. His eyes seemed unusually dull, more gray than blue . . . but it could have been a trick of the shadows.

"Please," he said, "hear me out?"

I nodded.

"I know you're upset, and I know why. I've been . . . well, I've been selfish lately. I'm not getting through this thing as well as I hoped I would." Lowering his eyes, he pulled in a shaky breath and then slowly let it out again. "That's no excuse to overlook your feelings, or what's important to you." He raised his eyes only halfway. "I'm sorry." I dismissed the Principle, and smiled. "We were both looking out for ourselves only," I said. "I'm sorry too."

"Friends?"

"I already told you, Judah . . . always."

"Like before?"

I nodded. "Count on it."

"I do," he said. "So . . . will you take your birthday present now?"

I grinned, then pretended to be offended. "You were pretty confident, weren't you?"

"No." He shook his head. "I was hopeful."

"Well?"

Smiling, he slid the small package out of his jacket pocket. "Rachel did wrap it," he said, "but I picked it out." He chuckled nervously. "You might not like it as well as something Rachel would have picked."

"I'll like it more." Gently, I removed the paper and lifted the lid of a square white box. With my forefinger, I raised a fine gold chain until its pendant caught a flash of sunlight—and my breath. Two hearts. Each trimmed in gold. One filled with Black Hills gold, the other with an amethyst. Overlapping. "Judah, it's beautiful," I said. "Will you help me put it on?"

His fingers, as he fumbled to clasp it, felt rough and warm against my skin—a pleasant contrast to the cool, fine chain. His smile when he pulled back to study me was the first real one I had seen in weeks.

"You're a good friend," he said. "The best."

"Hey, guys," a voice said behind us. "What are you doing up here?"

At first, I didn't recognize the voice and was afraid it might belong to a counselor who could too easily misinterpret the situation. But when he spoke again to ask us why we weren't at the lake, I relaxed. Fortunately, our lack of care to "avoid even the appearance of evil" wasn't going to get us in trouble.

But it could have. Yes, and my discomfort at that possibility was as valuable a deterrent as any reprimand.

"Because it's not that hot today," I told Nathan. "I don't like to swim unless it's really hot."

"And what do I want to do at the lake?" Judah asked, smiling. "When I try to swim, everyone else laughs."

"That's true." Nathan hissed, flailed his arms in the air, and yowled. "He's like a cat in the water."

"I am not!" Judah stood and pulled Nathan's arms down. "I just . . . never breathe at the right time."

We all laughed.

"Well," Nathan said, "you could sit in the tadpole section and splash people."

"Shut up." Still laughing, Judah shoved Nathan.

Nathan shoved him back, and that was it. Normally, this . . . need? . . . of even seemingly mature boys to get more grass stains on the other guy's jeans than he got on yours annoyed me, but not today. Not in these boys. It was good to see them laughing together.

When Nathan yelled, "Okay, okay! You can sit on the shore," Judah let him up, and we started walking down the hill toward the lake.

Judah was still brushing pine needles off his sleeves when we got to the grassy clearing at the far end of the lake. "I wonder what—"

"Hey, Ewen!" someone shouted to us from the water.

"Michael," Nathan muttered.

"Jump in, Nathan," Michael called. "Race you to the dock."

Nathan shook his head. "Not today."

"What's the matter? Afraid you'll lose?"

Several of Michael's friends laughed.

Nathan said nothing.

"Well, that's okay," Michael said. "I was getting out, anyway."

"He is so irritating," Nathan complained under his breath.

"Ignore him," Judah said.

When Michael stood to wade out of the water, one of the weeds that floated on the surface on this corner of the lake hung from his shoulder. He moved to shove it off, but stopped. "Hey guys," he said to his friends in a deep voice, "I'm a zombie from the deep!" He hunched like a ghoul and splashed as he stepped ashore. "I've drowned and come looking for the fool who let me die!"

His friends laughed. Some of them even grabbed weeds of their own and joined Michael on the beach.

To Michael's friends, this was an innocent—stupid, but innocent—game of Zombie. To Michael, it was another opportunity to harass Judah the way he had been all summer.

Judah, Nathan, and I kept walking.

"Rraaaah!" Michael moaned. "Out of my cold grave at last."

The other zombies agreed.

"Now for the fool who let me die!"

Nathan stopped walking. "This goes beyond irritation," he said. "I'm about to—"

"No." Slowly, Judah turned around and stepped a few feet away from us. He waited there for Michael to approach him.

And he did, even though his friends stayed near the water, swinging their weeds and chasing one another.

Why is Michael doing this? I wondered, not for the first time. He had certainly figured out by now that Judah was not going to tell Pastor Ewen about it . . . and why would he want that, anyway? His persistence in it convinced me that he was after something more than a laugh, but . . . what?

"Pretty good effects, huh?" When Michael stopped in front of Judah, he lifted the lake weed from his shoulder, held it in Judah's face for a moment, and then tossed it into the grass. He attempted a hideous, deep-throated laugh, but his regular one quickly interrupted it.

"You're not going to win, Michael."

I wasn't sure I knew exactly what Judah meant, but Michael seemed to. His face went serious, and his eyes, angry. "Do you ever think about it, Ewen?" he asked quietly. "The way your friend died?"

After staring at Michael for several long seconds, Judah stepped back on the trail and hurried past Nathan and me.

Michael followed him. "What was his last thought? Do you ever think about that? I bet it was something like, 'This wouldn't be happening if—' "

"Stop!" Judah spun around and glared at Michael. "Okay? Stop."

Michael grinned. He had finally squeezed a reaction out of Judah. "Or what?"

"Or *this!*" Nathan lunged at Michael, pushed him to the ground, and hit him. Twice. Three times.

Michael's friends dropped their weeds and ran toward us.

"Nathan, stop," I yelled.

But he didn't, and ten or fifteen kids watched the pastor's son break Michael's nose.

"Nathan," Judah whispered when his brother stood and left Michael alone to whine about his face, "you just—" He stopped, raised his hand to his mouth, and ran toward the trees.

"I just *what?*" Nathan shouted after him.

Suddenly, I knew. I grabbed Nathan's arm and pulled him away from Michael so the other kids wouldn't hear me. "You just gave Michael what he's wanted all along."

"Yeah. Sure."

"Think about it," I urged him. "Nathan, you *hit* him. Pastors' kids don't do that. Do you think enough of the men on our board are going to care about *why* you did it? No. They're just waiting for a reason to call a vote and get your dad out of there." I closed my eyes. "And now they have it."

"If that's true," he said, "I've just destroyed everything that Judah has put up with—three months of . . . of . . ."

He did not need to finish.

"What's going on here?" Pastor James demanded as he approached us on the trail followed by our youth pastor and the boy who had gone to get them.

"I hit him because . . . I was stupid," Nathan said.

Michael, who had finally gotten to his feet, shouted, "He broke my nose, man!"

"We can see that," said Pastor Dave. He turned to Pastor James. "These are both my kids," he said. "Can I take care of this?"

It took a moment, but Pastor James nodded. Before he left, he ordered all the kids who were not directly involved to find something else to do, including me.

Poor Pastor Dave, I thought as I walked toward the trees to find Judah. He had arrived at camp that morning expecting the usual youth camp fun and ministry, and he was about to find out that our church might be looking for its sixth pastor.

And Pastor Ewen. If only we had told him . . .

My misjudgment, my decision not to tell Pastor Ewen after Michael's first prank in the mall and after every prank since then, was as much a part of this outcome as Nathan's fist in Michael's face. I knew that. And the knowledge hurt.

Especially when I saw Judah.

His face was as gray as the rock he was sitting on.

I sat beside him and touched his hair lightly with my fingers. "Hey," I said, feeling as competent as the dirt at our feet to help him.

"It's too much," he whispered. "All of it. I said I would tell you. I can keep my word, at least." When he looked at me, I saw in his eyes the battle between the spirit that would face anything head-on and conquer it, and the fear and imposed insecurity that labored to cripple and defeat him. At this moment, the latter was winning, and he knew it. "I loved Tommy, Rebekah. I wanted . . . I . . . you know, but I can't . . . anymore. I need it finished."

"I know you do." I pulled him close to me and held him. He wasn't sobbing. He wasn't shaking. He wasn't even holding on to me. He just leaned against me, heavy, like a dead man.

It should have been finished in Alaska.

"It will be finished, Judah," I told him. "Soon."

Chapter Sixteen

"Beck?" Elly opened my bedroom door a crack. "You've been in here all day. Want to talk?"

"Talking makes me cry."

She stepped over my still unpacked suitcase and pulled open my curtains. "Looks like you've been doing that anyway." Pushing aside several crumpled tissues, she sat on my bed beside me. "I know you're upset about what happened at camp, but this is ridiculous."

"Go away."

"Why did Judah get so upset, anyway? Sure, pretending to be a zombie is pretty disgusting, but that's just Michael."

I lay down on my side and pulled my knees to my chest. "Go away."

"It must have made him think of his friend who drowned or something. You know, the one in Rachel's photo album." My stuffed white kitty seemed to cringe in her arms when she picked it up to hug it. "Still," she said, "it's nothing to lose your lunch over." She grinned. "Literally or figuratively."

I bolted to my door and yanked it open. "You don't know anything. Get out."

After squeezing my kitty, she tossed it on the bed and rose. "Don't I? Clue me in, then."

"Get *out!*"

"I know one thing," she said. "Judah's a wimp. He totally lost it over a game. Everyone knows it."

I stepped toward her. "They don't know anything."

"Mark and Corey were there, Beck, remember? After Pastor Dave left to take Nathan and Michael home, Corey told us—"

"Corey doesn't know anything."

"He was right there, Beck." Elly shook her head. "Judah's a wimp. Don't go losing your heart over it."

Part of me wanted to shove her out of my room, slam the door behind her, and forget she existed. The other part wanted to shout at her. The latter part won.

"You've got a lot of nerve, Elizabeth, sauntering in here and saying that to me when you don't know anything about it except what Corey *thinks* he knows. Do you think it matters to me in the slightest what you think of Judah? It doesn't. Is this your idea of cheering someone up? Get out!"

When she did not move, I pointed toward my door and screamed it. *"Get out!"*

"What's going on in here?"

My doorway was suddenly filled with Dad. I snapped my mouth shut and turned away from him.

"Beck?"

I said nothing, refusing to face him even when he tugged at my sleeve.

"Elly?"

Sighing, Elly dropped into my desk chair. "Dad, she's been sitting in here in the dark since we got home last night. I was trying to point out that it's stupid to get all depressed about what happened at camp."

"Why don't you tell him how you said it, Elly?"

"Okay." That arrogant slant at the right corner of her mouth appeared. "Judah's a wimp. W-I-M-P. Wimp. Better?"

When Dad finally spoke, his words were steady and controlled, his voice quiet, but rigid with intensity. "I can see how you and other kids would think that, Elly, since you don't know the whole story. You don't even know the *beginning* of the story. I cannot see how you can walk in here and say it to your sister when you do know how she feels about him."

"Dad—"

"I'm not done."

It had been years since Dad had used those words with that tone. Elly closed her mouth.

"I suspect that a lot of garbage will be going around the next few days," he said. "I want you to listen to the truth, remember it, and behave accordingly." He told Elly everything, and when he finished, glancing at me with something between concern and accusation, he left us alone to resolve our own battle.

"I'm sorry, Beck," Elly said. "I had no clue."

"Yeah, well, I made some big mistakes in this thing." I sat on the edge of my bed again. "Maybe not telling you was one of them."

She ran her forefinger along the spiral binding of my journal. "Don't be hard on yourself, Beck. Nobody would have expected Michael to be so . . . crude."

"I guess." I couldn't even make myself *sound* convinced.

Elly didn't press it. "Come on," she said. "Go get dressed and get some food in your stomach. Tonight's the Back-To-School-Pizza-Bash at youth group."

"I'm not going."

"Beck, you—"

"Why would I want to go there, Elly? Use your brain."

Slowly, she opened my door. "In case Judah's there?"

"That isn't likely."

"Not impossible, either." Stepping into the hall, she smiled. "He's not a wimp. Maybe he'll think he needs to prove it."

"Yeah . . . okay."

As we rode to church, though, I prayed that Judah would stay home. He did not need any more grief, and I was not convinced that Michael would be content with the damage he had already caused.

But Judah was there, standing in the entryway with Nathan and Rachel while Pastor Dave hauled in the pizzas.

Elly approached them with me. "You guys okay?" she asked.

They all nodded.

"So, what happens now?"

I wanted to elbow my sister but I stood still. It was a legitimate question. I only wished she had not asked it in front of Judah.

"Up to the board," Nathan replied. "Dad's going to talk to Mr. Kramer. Everyone's upset I broke Michael's nose. It's stupid, but that's the way people are."

"They'll either side with Dad or Mr. Kramer," Rachel added. "That's what it will all come down to."

I cringed. It did not require supernatural ability to predict that outcome. "Let's go get some pizza, eh?"

We walked as a group toward the fellowship hall.

"Judah?"

He looked quickly over his shoulder.

Behind us, Natalie Potts stood alone, clutching her jacket in trembling hands. "I. . ." She cleared her throat. "When I told my father what happened at camp, he—"

"Save it, Natalie." Elly grabbed Judah's arm to lead him away.

He shook Elly's hand away and turned to fully face Natalie. "Go ahead."

"He told me about your friend and . . . well, I understood then why. . . . Anyway, I'm sorry." Her eyes closed as she breathed out slowly. "I want you to know that I . . . I'm for you guys. So's my dad."

"Thanks." Judah didn't smile, but his eyes communicated what this meant to him. "Really, Natalie. Thanks."

When Natalie nodded and walked ahead of us into the fellowship hall, Elly said, "Maybe the rest of the board will use their heads too and vote out Mr. Kramer instead of your father."

"Let's hope they can . . . get through this without voting anyone out."

As we approached the serving table, Michael Kramer stepped in front of us. Receiving glares from all of us but Judah, he smiled broadly. Strings of mozzarella cheese dangled from the corners of his mouth, and he took his time about slurping them back in. Then he said, "You aren't sore at me, are you, Judah? I mean, I was just playing around, and I'm the one whose nose is out of joint over it." He bit off a third of his slice of pizza.

Pastor Dave stopped talking to Steve Alton. "Go sit down, Mr. Kramer."

"How about it, Ewen?" Michael wiped his hand on his jeans and extended it to Judah. "No hard feelings."

Judah neither spoke nor moved to clasp Michael's hand, but Nathan did move. He stepped in front of Judah to stand right in Michael's face. Though two inches shorter, he forced Michael back two steps with his unyielding glare. "I've been thinking," he said, "that it really can't hurt much if I rearrange your teeth too."

"Nathan, don't." Judah placed his hand on his brother's shoulder. "It's okay. Keep your temper."

"You listen to Mom too much, Judah. You might be willing to stand around while this jerk gets his laughs, but I'm not." Nathan stepped closer to Michael. "Not now."

"This isn't the way I want to win this."

Nathan's anger turned with his body away from Michael and plowed into Judah. "How *do* you intend to win this? The poor martyr thing? Divine intervention? Why don't you defend yourself? It doesn't matter now, anyway."

"Because he's not worth it."

I wasn't sure when, but everyone had stopped talking. Pizza slices lay half eaten on paper plates.

We looked to Pastor Dave, and he did not waste time. "Nathan, go outside and cool off," he said, grabbing Nathan's right arm and forcibly directing him toward the door.

Unfortunately, Nathan had lost his mood to heed authority, reason, or anything else. He tore his arm free of Pastor Dave's grip and asked Judah, as if he'd never been interrupted, "What are you trying to prove? You've let this fool stomp over you all summer. That's fine. There was reason then. Now there's no more reason. Now you can—"

"There is reason," Judah said quietly.

"What reason?"

"My testimony," Judah said simply. "I'm not willing to offend God because of him."

Nathan's mouth hung open for a moment, then slowly closed. The entire room was silent, waiting. Even Michael stopped chewing his pizza to ponder the point.

His *testimony.* Something, but for a few bouts of quiet moodiness (and forgetting my birthday), that he had almost flawlessly maintained.

But . . . at what cost?

Apparently, Nathan had been asking himself the same question. He moved a step back from Judah. "No, Judah," he said, mocking. "You haven't lost your testimony." His eyes narrowed and his jaw tightened so that his next words spit out through clenched teeth. "Only your mind."

Michael laughed, but he stopped because nobody joined him.

The battle between Judah's will and his emotion raged plainly in his face as he fought to steady it. Quickly, deliberately, he said, "I'm going home."

When Judah turned and left, Nathan took off after him. I barely caught the back of his sweatshirt as he tried to run by me. "Nathan," I pleaded, "let him go. Just . . . let him go."

Reluctantly, Nathan obeyed.

Pastor Dave and Rachel went after Judah instead. Nathan stood in the entryway for several minutes, and then left too.

"What a messed up family." Michael leaned smugly against the serving table and shook his head.

Natalie snatched the slice of pizza out of Michael's hand and slapped it onto his face. "You're such a jerk."

"Better be careful, Natalie," Elly said. "Your dad could end up looking for a new job."

"Guys," I stammered, wanting to laugh, cry, and throw up all at once, "let's put some music on and try to have some fun. This is a party. We . . . we're Christians." I handed Michael a napkin. "There's an olive stuck on your bandage."

Everyone laughed then, more out of relief than because anything was funny. Gradually, the party regained its noisy momentum. The chitchat seemed strained, but at least it had begun again. When Pastor Dave returned and introduced the first game of the evening, nearly everyone was behaving as if nothing had happened.

Everyone but the leadership kids.

I had to get out of there.

"Beck?" Elly and Natalie followed me into the hallway. "You were great."

For some reason, I started laughing and couldn't stop. Maybe it was the image of Natalie Potts smearing pizza all over Michael's ugly face. Maybe it was the olive. Maybe it was because if I didn't laugh, I would die.

Elly hugged me.

That's when I cried. Hard. "I can't stop thinking that they're going to leave. What will I do if he leaves?" *I may as well say it,* I decided. "I've never felt . . . the way I feel about him."

"Is that supposed to be news?" Elly laughed. "I've heard that long-distance romances are the best kind." Gently, she pushed some hair back away from my face.

I shook my head.

She hugged me tighter. "Beck, it'll be better for him somewhere else, you know? He needs to get over this thing, and he obviously can't do that here."

It was too much to reason through at that moment, so I nodded just to appease her.

"Think of it this way," Natalie said, smiling. "Every afternoon you rush to the mailbox, hoping for that special something with a Montana postmark—or wherever they go. You leaf frantically through your parents' junk mail until you find it. When you do, you dump everything else on the driveway and dash to your room to open it."

Elly giggled. "First, you kiss the back of the envelope where he would have kissed it when he sealed it."

"Shut up," I whispered, hoping they would ignore me.

They didn't.

"Beck," Elly said, her face serious beneath a gentle smile, "if it's what God wants for you and Judah, He can make it work even if they do leave."

Pastor and Mrs. Ewen's unlikely reunion long ago in South America testified to that plainly enough, but . . .

"And if Judah isn't the one God wants for you, then—"

"I know," I said, waving my hand. "I know."

In unison, Elly and I placed our hands on our hips, tilted our heads to the left—just a bit—the way Mom always did, and said, "You shouldn't want it, either."

But I did want it, more than anything.

And I didn't want letters from Montana.

Chapter Seventeen

"Rick, I'm at my wit's end."

It was Wednesday. Raining. Dad had just let Pastor Ewen in the front door. I had been at the kitchen table all morning. My hot chocolate had gone cold an hour ago, and my sheet of paper, on which I had intended to write a letter to Allison, was still blank except for the date.

"I went to the Kramers on Monday to apologize for Nathan, since he refuses to do it himself," Pastor Ewen explained, without waiting for Dad to close the door or offer him a chair.

Dear Allison, I wrote, trying to concentrate on my own business instead of Pastor Ewen's. *How are you?*

"I wanted to assure them I'd pay Michael's doctor bills," Pastor Ewen continued. "That was fine with them, and they showed me to the door."

I picked up my pencil again. *I've been better. We start school Monday.*

"When I asked Joe how Michael knew about Tommy, he got offended. Said he certainly didn't tell him. Michael says Nathan told him. I know that's not true, Rick. Things aren't the best between Nathan and Judah all the time, but Nathan wouldn't have done that. But, what could I say to Joe? I'd be calling his son a liar."

Camp was . . . I erased that. Allison did not need to know how camp had been. *How's your dad?*

"Rick, they didn't even bother to ask about Judah. The kid won't eat. He can't sleep. He doesn't talk to you unless you specifically ask him something, and sometimes not even then. Esther is set to start packing. Nathan's steaming that I'd pay Michael's bills. Rachel is . . ."

Rachel says hi. She got a job at the art museum.

"Me? I'm so angry I can't even think straight, let alone try to hear God about it. Michael. Joe and Nancy. My kids. Judah, even. Judah must think this church is more important to me than he is. It isn't, Rick, and he should know that after last time."

Church is . . . well . . . What was I doing? Talk about handing Allison an excuse to ignore my advice about finding a church. I crinkled the letter and tossed it in the garbage.

This wasn't going to work.

"Mostly, though, I'm angry with myself." The heaviness in Pastor Ewen's voice alarmed me. If the situation had beaten *him* down to this level of hopelessness, who would be left standing to remedy it? He was the pastor.

"I know what it means when Judah reads all the time," he said. "When he's quiet . . . He's my son. I should have been paying attention."

"Ben—"

"I'm sorry, Rick. I didn't come here to whine. I came to see if you had the time to come pray with me this afternoon before the service tonight. God's the only one who knows what I'm meant to do with all this. I just . . . I need someone in the gap with me here."

Dad replied quickly, sincerely. "Of course I have time."

The two men left the house. I heard the door close behind them and Pastor Ewen's Jeep start and pull away.

They were going to ask wisdom from God.

He's the only one who knows . . .

But, what if God's answer wasn't one I wanted? What if He actually wanted the Ewens in Timaru, New Zealand, or somewhere? What if He wanted them back in Alaska? And, what if His answer was a long time in coming? What if, in the meantime, Judah became so frustrated with things that a leap from a bridge seemed a more workable finish? What if, like our last pastor, Ben Ewen decided that our church simply wasn't worth the drain on his family, and resigned? What if . . . ?

For the rest of that week, these questions and countless others toyed with my mind so that, by Sunday morning, my head ached as much as my heart, and I just wanted it over. No matter what *over* meant.

At least, that's what I thought.

"Beck, when you get a minute, I need to talk to you."

"Just a second, Dad," I called back, leaning into the hallway so he would hear me in the den. Three women. One bathroom. A car that left for church at exactly nine o'clock when everyone had overslept. A typically imperfect Sunday morning, but worse. Elly was hogging the mirror, my hair was opposing my plans for it, and Mom had just gagged us with an explosive gust of perfume—Sea Mist, or something.

"Beck? Now, please."

"Okay, Dad, I'm coming." Straight hair was going to have to suffice, I decided, dropping my brush down onto the counter.

As I hurried toward the den, my tension turned to something so close to dread that I could feel it on the back of my neck. The strain in Dad's face when he met me in the doorway did nothing to relieve it. "Are you sick?" I asked him, almost hoping he'd say yes.

"No. You knew we were having a board meeting while you kids were in youth church last night?"

I shook my head. "I thought it was next week."

"It was early."

This was not a comforting bit of information.

"Well," Dad said, "it—"

The telephone rang.

Dad answered it, spoke with someone in mostly yes's and no's, and hung up. "Beck," he said, approaching me again, "Ben—"

Another blaring ring from the phone ushered Dad into a second yes, no, it's true, I'm sorry too, conversation. When he finished, he held the receiver in his hand instead of hanging it up. "Beck, Ben—"

His watch alarm beeped. Nine o'clock.

"Don't tell me, Dad," I said.

"Beck—"

"Don't." I kissed his cheek. "I'm a big girl. I'll find out with everyone else."

Dad let it go, but as we rode to church in silence, I could muster no doubt—though I tried—that there were only two possible results of last night's board meeting that he would feel compelled to forewarn me about. Pastor Ewen had been voted out, or he had resigned. Either way, it meant the same thing for me, and I didn't want to think about it.

When we arrived, Dad led us quickly past the group of anxious board members who had gathered in the entryway. "Sit with me today," he said to Elly and me.

We did not argue.

I followed him to the front row, where we sat beside Pastor and Mrs. Ewen. Pastor Ewen offered a greeting, and Mrs. Ewen only nodded at us. Their kids were not at church.

Though Mr. Kramer made a show of being regretful about claiming the pulpit when it was time, I suspected that beneath his serious face he was a living exclamation mark. He held the sober expression through the opening prayer and for a quiet moment afterwards as he scanned the assembly. "I stand before you this morning with a very unpleasant task," he said.

When I knew he would see me, I scrunched my face in distaste. The least he could do was spare us the trite garbage.

"Your church government is balanced between a pastor and a board," he said. "Usually, this encourages a team effort in working for your benefit, each side checking and sustaining the other."

Speak in English. One pastor. Nine remaining board members. Balanced? Not exactly.

"Sadly, this has not been the case with Pastor Ewen."

Right.

"Pastors are men. They fail. They sin. They mishear God. Sometimes it is our function as the other half of church government to—and it's never easy—weigh this out and determine whether our church is being hurt by him rather than served. If this is the case, then it is our duty to . . ."

Elect Joe Kramer as pastor?

". . . insure your best interests."

Mr. Kramer was smooth. Grieved eyes, but not too grieved. Just enough remorse and trepidation in his tone. Perfect to convince people that he had labored hours in prayer over this thing, and now, though it's nearly killing him to do it, he's standing in what God has called him to do. For us, of course.

I was glad I had not eaten breakfast.

"Please turn in your Bibles to I Timothy chapter three."

I could not look at Pastor Ewen. What must he be feeling? I wondered, as I suspected he did, why God had allowed him to come to us at all when He knew it would end in injustice.

"Begin at verse one," Mr. Kramer continued flatly from the pulpit. "*This is a true saying, If a man desire the office of a bishop, he desireth a good work. A bishop then must be blameless, the husband of one wife, vigilant, sober, of good behavior, given to hospitality, apt to teach; Not given to wine, no striker, not greedy of filthy lucre; but patient, not a brawler, not covetous . . .*" Mr. Kramer glanced up at us. "In all this, Ben Ewen is qualified. More than qualified, in fact. But let's go on. *One that ruleth well his own house, having his children in subjection with all gravity; (For if a man know not how to rule his own house, how shall he take care of the church of God?)*"

Leaning heavily against the podium, Mr. Kramer closed his Bible. "We, the board, have deemed it necessary, in response to actions by two of Ben's kids, to evaluate him in light of this last criterion, and, regretfully, find him lacking."

My hands tightened around my Bible.

"One might point out, as Ben did," Mr. Kramer went on, "that kids are kids and will make mistakes. This is certainly true. Any parent knows that. But we aren't talking about minor slip-ups, here. Disrespect and flagrant violence. Must we excuse any action on the basis of youth? I think not. That's why this Scripture is here. Children are brought up by parents. Children take their example from their parents. Children become what their parents are——"

"That explains why Michael is such a jerk, *sir.*"

Everyone behind and around me gasped. I turned in horror to look at Elly.

"Why don't you tell everyone why Nathan broke Michael's nose?" My sister stood up to further challenge Mr. Kramer. "I think that would shed a whole lot of——"

Pastor Ewen stood, suggested to Elly—with a firm hand on the shoulder—that she sit down, and said, "Can I say something, Joe?"

Mr. Kramer nodded, but made no move to surrender the pulpit or his microphone.

Needing neither, Pastor Ewen addressed us. "As a pastor, a man must be prepared to put up with a lot from people. I am prepared to be opposed for my stands on certain issues. And, to a certain extent, I am prepared to allow my family to endure some unpopularity also. I was not prepared for what happened at this church. Neither were they."

Mr. Kramer cleared his throat and straightened as if he intended to speak, but Pastor Ewen wasn't finished.

"I'm not going to get into a discussion of who did what to whom first," he said, "because, frankly, it doesn't matter. Joe's right. What

Nathan did to Michael is inexcusable, no matter how under-standable it seems to some of us. I'm not interested in defending myself or fighting for my position. I am interested in apologizing to you—the church. Not for my sons, but for myself and this board. We have failed, since the day I arrived, to work as a team."

They didn't give you a chance, Pastor Ewen.

"Is this my fault?" he asked. "Theirs? Does it matter anymore? What does matter is you, and the fact that we have all failed you by not pressing together toward whatever it was that God put me in this place to do. I did not come here intending to fail, and I repent to you that we did." Slowly, he turned to face Mr. Kramer. "I spoke with Pastor Fenton this morning. He's going to come and take this church until the problems that were not caused by me can be sorted out and corrected."

A flicker of concern—or was it alarm?—shook Mr. Kramer's arrogance, narrowing his eyes slightly, but he squelched it quickly behind a belittling smirk.

Pastor Ewen faced us again. "As for my family and me, I figure we'll make a trip of heading back up to Montana. I've got to work through some things with my kids that I realize I've neglected. And we'll see what God has for us after that." He smiled. "Real sheep, maybe. Or selling unbreakable china door to door."

Quiet laughter rippled through the congregation.

The kind of laughter meant to trap tears inside.

"We'll be here for a couple of weeks packing up," Pastor Ewen said too matter-of-factly. This was killing him, and we all knew it. But he was tough. "You'll see us around. I want you all to remember, especially now, that God is sovereign. He will continue to be faithful to you even though you were let down by us. I don't believe for a moment that this end was ever His intention, but He can, and *will,* use it for good . . . somehow. We can, and must, have confidence in that. In Him."

All around me, as Pastor Ewen reached for his wife's hand and left the sanctuary with her, people were crying.

I cried.

How could God have authored this? Was I expected to believe that it was His will for our church to get a pastor, destroy him, toss him out, and get a new one, like kids do with shoes, again and again and again?

Of course not.

But, if this was not God's will, why was He allowing it to happen? When was He going to put His foot down? What about His promises?

I didn't know. I believed them, but I also knew that God was going to have to do some serious intervention to see any of this work together for good.

Our pastor was leaving.

Our friends.

Chapter Eighteen

Judah wouldn't talk to me.

Every afternoon, I'd sit with him on the Ewens' porch steps, telling him about my classes, my teachers, that Jeremy said hello, and asking him if he had ever seen a more dramatic sunset.

He would say nothing.

His icy wall of silence unnerved me, but I knew it would have to give way sooner or later, and I wanted to be there for him when it did.

Mrs. Ewen raised a gloved hand to me when I walked up their gravel driveway Friday afternoon. Getting up stiffly from the patch of garden she had been weeding, she pulled off her gardening gloves and approached me. "Come in and have some iced tea," she said. "Judah's upstairs. Sleeping."

"That's progress," I said, smiling as I followed her inside. Immediately, I wished I had waited outside. Packed, half-packed, and not-yet-assembled moving cartons cluttered the floor so that we had to step over and around them on our way back to the kitchen. Though I had known that the Ewens were leaving, seeing these boxes turned the concept into its harsh reality. "When are you pulling out?" I asked Mrs. Ewen, forcing a casualness I didn't feel.

"Next Sunday," she said. "We'll say our good-byes at the church outing on Saturday, and leave early Sunday morning."

The annual church picnic at Silver Canyon Park. I had forgotten about it. "Eight days," I muttered.

"Not a lot of time, is it?"

Mrs. Ewen and I turned together to see Judah standing in the doorway. I wanted to smile because he had finally said something, but I couldn't because he still looked so worn.

"I think," he said, stepping toward me, "that I still owe you an ice-cream cone. Sound good?"

It did.

"We'll stop at the church on our way back," he told his mother as we left. "We can help Rachel load up Dad's books."

"She'll appreciate that," Mrs. Ewen said.

Judah and I walked two blocks without speaking.

Three.

When the silence began to intimidate me, I said, "Elly likes her classes at the college."

"Yeah?"

"Um hmm. She's taking—" I did not want to talk about Elly. "Judah, we only have eight days. The last thing I want to spend the time discussing is my sister."

"I'm sorry. I've . . . I've been pretty bad company."

"It's okay. I understand." I stepped closer to him.

"It's not okay. People have gone through tougher things and kept themselves together better."

"You're always so hard on yourself, Judah."

"Because I wanted to do this God's way. You know, patiently. Not barely-hanging-in-there, stressed-out patient, but *joyful* patient. All the way through to the end of it. I'm trying, but I'm not getting it right. I mean, I feel like I'm walking on a long, narrow log a few feet above the edge of a cliff, and if someone pushes, even slightly, I'll either fall over the edge or come down on them. I don't want to do either. I want to be able to smile, keep my balance, and walk on. Does that make any sense, or is Nathan right about me losing my mind?"

"It makes sense."

I had feared his shutting me out, but now that he was inviting me further into his heart than I had ever been, I wondered what I could really do to help. Nothing, most likely, and I loathed the realization. "Why don't you talk to your dad? He wants you to. You don't have to deal with this alone."

Shaking his head, he said, "I can't face him without thinking of everything I've cost him. Can you understand that? The church he pioneered. His friendship with Tommy's father. This church. I mean, he's got to be wishing I had gone with Tommy, even if it was only to drown with him."

I stopped walking. Grabbing both of his arms, I made him turn to face me. "Don't ever say that. Ever. Your father loves you. More than his churches." I released him, angry. "You should know that."

His eyes seemed to drain of strength right there in front of me, but he did not try to escape my stare. "I'm sorry," he said. "I do know that. I'm sorry."

We started walking again, silently, and not so close to each other. Past the ice-cream shop.

"You can talk to me," I said. "You know that."

His stride quickened. "I want to. I do. But—"

"I'm not promising I'll have answers, but I do have ears."

"Pretty ones." He smiled for only an instant. "Since that day at camp, I keep thinking about what Michael asked me . . . if I've ever thought about the way Tommy died. I have. A lot. The water and the cold . . . and all. I hope it . . . was fast. He shouldn't have been alone to die."

I shuddered to think I had invited this. "You're right," I said, and then hurried to explain before he could misinterpret. "He should have been with you. On the trail. That's where he should have been. It isn't your fault that he wasn't."

"But it is my fault I wasn't with him."

"Try to think of it this way, okay? Say you and I get married and—"

He smiled.

"Stop." I felt the heat in my cheeks but ignored it. "Listen. We're married and Allison wants me to come to New York to . . . help her with her wedding, or something. Anyway, while I'm there, we go into the city to do some of the shopping. The guy at our hotel specifically tells us not to venture out at night because the neighborhood is unsafe. You know Allison. She decides it would be educational to see some real-life thugs, hookers, and gangs, and suggests a stroll. I refuse, of course, but she insists that she's going whether I go or not. If I called for your advice, what would you tell me?"

He thought for a long moment. Half a block long. "I wouldn't let you go to New York without me."

"Be serious. I'm rebellious and went anyway."

"You? No way." He grinned. "But, for the sake of your point, I'd tell you to try to keep her home."

"If she refused?"

"Let her go alone."

"Even though with two of us the chances of something happening would be less?"

"Not enough less to risk my beautiful wife."

"So, I should just . . . send her out to—"

"I know what you're trying to make me do, Rebekah, but it's not the same thing."

I sighed. "Okay. What's different?"

He raised his hands to press at his temples. "Well, violent people are a lot harder to predict and manage than a river we had crossed twenty times before, for one thing, and—"

"Let's do one thing at a time," I said, lifting my hand to interrupt him. "You can't swim. I assume Tommy could?"

He nodded.

"He drowned in that river. That predictable, manageable river. What could you have done, Judah, even if you had been there?"

"I could have tossed him a rope."

"Did you have a rope? Handy?"

"Handy enough, Rebekah."

I bit my bottom lip. This was an argument I needed to win. Convincingly. If he stumped me, it would only cement his reasoning. I would not allow that. Could not.

"See," he said, "the thing is, I don't know what happened. Why Tommy came off his horse. I don't know any of that. I don't know what I would have done, but he wouldn't have been alone. I'd have been there, and I would have done *something* . . . whatever I needed to do."

"I know you would have," I said. "Even if it came down to jumping in that river yourself to try to help him. But, Judah, you can't swim. Most likely, you'd be dead now too."

When he stopped walking and turned to face me, the untouched pain and self-condemnation in his eyes warned me that I was treading on raw hurt. "I'd have tried, though," he said, the words barely audible. "A friend wouldn't have let him go alone."

"Those are not your words, Judah." I stared back at him, just as fiercely, with just as much conviction. "Those are Mr. Cook's words. Mr. Kramer's, maybe. You believe them, but they aren't true. Listen to your own words to me. 'Try to keep her from going, but don't go yourself.' Remember? That's what you would tell me. That's what you did. What happened to Tommy was his own fault—if it has to be anyone's. Just like it would be if Allison went out and got mugged, or even killed."

Visibly annoyed, Judah clutched the top board of the fence we had been passing and stared down at the mud beneath it. "This is not the sort of thing you can work out in your head like a neat little math problem. Someone is dead. My friend. Nathan's friend. People blame me, Rebekah. I can't just settle for what you're saying."

"Hardly anyone blames you," I said, unwilling to lose any of the ground I hoped I had gained. "Only a few people. People who can't see past their own grief enough to realize that sometimes there is nobody to—"

"They matter!"

Across the street, a screen door whacked shut as an elderly woman stepped onto her porch and stared curiously at Judah and me. We should have been having this discussion at the church or at one of our houses, with his father, not alone in the middle of the seven hundred block of Bethel Road.

"Judah—"

"Tommy's dad. Enough of Dad's friends to force him to resign his church. Michael."

"Don't be stupid!" I had not intended to speak so harshly to him . . . but wasn't it justified? "Who cares what Michael thinks? He doesn't care about Tommy. He's just trying to—"

"Nathan."

Nathan.

Now we were getting somewhere, and I knew exactly which way to take it. "Nathan doesn't blame you for Tommy's death. He and I talked about it after my dad—"

"He *does* blame me that Dad lost his church, though. Church*es*. He thinks that if I'd been tougher, like him, it would have been different."

"Yeah." I laughed cynically. "Then your father would be out because *you* broke Michael's nose . . . if that's what he means by toughness."

"It isn't." Closing his eyes and breathing in hard, Judah raised his hands to his face, held them there for several seconds, and then slid them back through his hair. "We'd better go straight to the church or we'll miss Rachel," he said.

"Don't push me away like that, Judah."

"I'm not trying to." He placed his hands on my shoulders and pulled me close to him. "It just . . . it won't make any difference, talking about Nathan. Why bog through it? He and I are different. Probably always will be. He doesn't think much of me, and I can't blame him. There's nothing left to talk about. Okay? Please."

"Okay." I stood there, overwhelmed. Had I really been so girlishly foolish as to believe that I, Rebekah Cahill, could solve the problem that Pastor and Mrs. Ewen, and Judah himself, had been helpless to combat?

As we began to walk, Judah smiled at the elderly woman across the street. "You'll write me, won't you, when we're gone?" He turned to me, still smiling. "I'm not much good at letters."

Every bit of strength that had helped me stand tough in Judah's grief now abandoned me. My face grew hot, then cold, then hot again, as everything from my throat to the pit of my stomach tightened around my heart. I squeezed my eyes shut, but tears came anyway—cold on my hot cheeks and warm on my cold fists as I swiped at them. Then Judah was holding me tightly against his black sweater, telling me to trust him, it wasn't the end of the world. He sounded as unconvinced of that as I felt, but he kept saying it, again and again until I wiped my eyes, pulled away from him, and mumbled something about being okay now.

We both laughed without emotion when the elderly woman's screen door squeaked open and shut again. *Fwak.*

"She's calling the police," Judah whispered. "We're disturbing the peace."

"I didn't notice any peace to disturb," I said.

He smiled. "You've got to look up for that. We've only been looking around."

I nodded as we started walking again. We did not speak, but the silence seemed constructive in its own way.

When we arrived at the church a few minutes later, Rachel, who had stacked several boxes of books just inside the front doors, peeked around the corner. "Hey, you two," she said, smiling at me, "you're right on time." She carried a huge crate of books into the entryway, deposited it in Judah's arms, and dropped her car keys on top. "The trunk is already full. These'll have to go in the back seat. You can run them home and come back for us, okay?"

"And afterwards dinner, Ma'am?"

She smiled at her brother, then tilted her head back to squint down her nose at him. "Superb idea, Neville, truly superb." Laughing, she slapped Judah's back. "Take care of my car."

"I will."

After Judah had loaded up the boxes and driven away with them, Rachel pulled Pastor Ewen's office door shut and said, "Let's wait for him outside. Being in here makes me sad." She hung the cleaning rag in the utility closet and led me outside, locking the front door behind us. "I'm going to miss you, Rebekah." She hugged me. "Not as much as Judah, I'm sure, but a lot."

"Don't get me started." I giggled. "Poor Judah. Right in the middle of the street and I was crying like an idiot."

"I doubt he minded." She sat down on the top step. "You know, to be honest, leaving here doesn't bug me that much . . . except being sad for Dad and Judah. People here never really took me in or—"

"You're sad for Judah? I'm only surviving this because I keep telling myself it'll be better for him somewhere else."

"It will be," Rachel said. "But he'll miss you. You two have something special." She laughed. "I hate that word. Special. But it's true."

I nodded and fidgeted with my sandal strap. "I bet you're glad you didn't fall in love here, huh?"

"I forbade myself to even *think* about it until after Dad's six month evaluation thing," she said. "I just decided to wait it out."

"You were smart. I thought you guys would be here forever. Your dad's an awesome pastor. Who wouldn't want him to stay, right?"

She nodded, her eyes sad. "So you fell in love with my little brother."

My face answered for me.

"Don't be hard on yourself for not foreseeing the craziness that happened here. Judah's about as good as they come, even with everything he's fighting inside."

I nodded. She tapped my arm with the back of her hand. "I bet he has a date the day of his eighteenth birthday."

"Thanks, Rachel. The thought cheers me considerably."

She laughed. "Did I say it wouldn't be you?"

"No, but I think it's fairly obvious since you're all going to be in Montana, or God knows where, and I'm going to be here."

Her blue eyes lost their sadness as she smiled at me and shrugged. "Oh, I don't know, Rebekah. You never know."

Chapter Nineteen

The day was hot, and the car even more so. The forty-five-minute ride on the washboard gravel road which led to Silver Canyon Park was stifling. Around us, the forest grew closer together and taller, but was mostly obscured by the dust of the vehicles in front of us. I could see dust, taste it on my teeth, and smell it above pine, car exhaust, and the chocolate brownies on the seat beside me.

As the road worsened, however, and our driving speed slowed accordingly, the dust settled, allowing us glimpses of the rugged gray peaks and the river through the trees. Swift, strong, and savage, the river pulsed its way through the canyon it had carved. Mighty, and oblivious to us.

Silver Canyon Park was a small grassy oasis in the rock and water of the canyon floor. Wildflowers, grass, mountains, sun, and always, the roaring allure of the river. A fine place for a picnic, but I was not in the mood for food, fun, and fellowship.

When I said goodbye to the Ewens at the end of the day, it might be for years . . . maybe even forever.

I decided to go for a hike and invited the Ewen kids to join me. Nathan declined, wanting to stay for the volleyball game, but Judah and Rachel accepted gratefully, even after I warned them about the trail's narrow cliffside stretches that kept most people content to live without the view from the top of the peak.

"It passes a cave halfway up," I told them when we had walked about half a mile downstream.

"The river's loud," Judah said.

"Another quarter mile or so and we switchback up into the trees." I quickened my pace. This was going to get worse before it got better if the river was intimidating him. I hadn't thought of that . . . the way the river narrowed, sped up, and beat around bigger boulders as the rock wall rose up beside us. The sound of it and its echo between the two canyon walls was deafening at times.

Normally, I would have hopped out onto one of the flat boulders a few feet from shore to point out the raging water further downstream, but today I hurried past them all, around the corner and into the trees—away from the river.

We walked single file past a few trees, over a lot of rock, and carefully along the loose earth of an ancient rockslide. The river still roared as loudly, but now it was accompanied by the moan of the wind.

I wondered if Judah found this as romantic as I did—walking together into this howling tunnel of river and wind.

Probably not.

He was probably beginning to wish that he had stayed at the picnic area with everyone else. Church picnics are fun. He could have played volleyball, or joined in on the tug-of-war.

"This is gorgeous," Rachel said.

"It is," Judah agreed. "I'm glad—" He stopped walking. "Did you hear that?"

"What?" Rachel asked.

"I'm not sure. I heard something. Listen."

River and wind.

I listened a moment, then shrugged. "Let's go. It must have been a bird or—"

"Wait," Rachel said. "I just heard it. It sounded like a shout."

"A shout?"

As if cued by a starter's gun, we ran together back to where the trail had turned and scanned the water.

There *was* a yell. Then another. Words.

"Help! Somebody! Help!"

An arm lifted into the air behind one of the massive boulders that littered the opposite shoreline.

"Why doesn't he pull himself to shore?" Rachel wondered aloud. "It's not far, and it can't be too deep."

"Maybe he's hurt or stuck in some kind of crosscurrent." I stepped closer to the water, straining to see.

"Can you see who it is?"

Judah shook his head. "I can see he's got clothes on. He must have been hiking and fallen in." He walked to the edge of the water, into the spray of the current around a projecting tree root. "Hey," he shouted, "can you hear me?"

"Help!" The voice was masculine, but sharp with terror. "I think my leg's broken!" He lifted his head as if to look at us, but slid back into the water.

"We've got to do something," Judah yelled, panic gripping his voice and eyes.

"We will." Rachel rested her hand steadily on her brother's shoulder. "Stay calm, okay?" Only when she turned to me did she allow her fear to narrow her eyes. "Have you ever swum in a current like this? Across it?"

I had not.

The person groped and dragged himself onto another rock a few feet farther downstream.

"Hang on, okay?" Judah ran downstream on our side.

When the person lifted his head and shouted, "I'll try!" I got a good look at him.

Michael.

My heart relaxed in relief before tensing again in fury. "It's Michael." I swallowed hard. "You guys, it's *Michael.*" Even after everything he had done, this surprised me. Who could have predicted such reckless cruelty?

"Kramer," I shouted at him, "when you get out of that water and I can reach you, you're going to wish you had drowned. And I don't think my dad will mind losing his job over it, either!"

Judah ran to me. "Be glad it's him and not someone really in trouble," he said. "I don't care about the joke." He cupped his hands around his mouth and addressed Michael. "Very funny. Come out before you get hypothermia."

"I'm going to kill him myself," Rachel muttered. "What a . . ." She waved her hand, unable to think of—or unwilling to speak—the appropriate term.

"Jerk?" I supplied.

"That doesn't begin to—"

"Hey! Hey!" Michael slipped from his new rock and thrashed about in the water. "Hey! Help!"

With the corners of her mouth creased in disgust, Rachel marched past us, back toward the trail. "Let's go."

"I want to see him get out first," Judah said. "The water's real cold. He could get in trouble."

"Oh, who cares?"

Judah answered her with a sharp glance.

So we waited, Rachel and I watching in amusement, and Judah in undecided relief, as Michael pulled his torso over the rim of yet a third rock.

"It's not a joke," he insisted pathetically, coughing as if he had swallowed the entire Pacific Ocean. "I swear, man! My leg! Please. It's not a joke!"

"Right." I tugged at Judah's sleeve. "And I'm Queen Elizabeth."

Water splashed up around Michael as he flopped into the river again. Flailing his arms rapidly, he barely managed to keep his head above the surface. "I'm going to die in here! Ewen? It's cold!"

"He's scared." Judah spun around to address Rachel. "He's really scared."

Even as Rachel's eyes squinted in frustration with Judah's willingness to believe Michael, she stepped forward to comfort him. "Judah, it's *Michael.* Don't you think it's a little too convenient of him to fall in and drown right in front of you? With nobody else around? Come on, Judah. *Think.*"

"All I can think, Rachel, is that it might not be a joke. Then what?"

"It is." She turned away from him and kicked a tree.

Pushing his fingers anxiously through his hair, Judah hurried back to the shoreline. "Michael? Pal? If this is a joke, get out now, before someone really does get hurt. This isn't a smart place to look for a last laugh."

Spraying water danced on Michael's face as he stretched out halfway over another rock. "Judah," he gasped, "I know you think I'm just harassing you again, but you've got to believe me. I'm scared, man! My leg—"

After glancing at me, his eyes pleading me to tell him that this really was not happening, Judah stepped cautiously into the water.

I went after him. Chilling water soaked my jeans and plastered them to my calves. "What are you doing?"

"What does it look like?"

"Judah, please." Water rose above my knees and swirled around them after only six very small steps. Already trying to topple me. "Judah, it's Michael! Stop!"

"No."

"It's a joke."

But, what if Michael, intending a joke, had really fallen in and injured himself? What if his life truly was in jeopardy?

Not a chance.

"You don't know that any more than I do, Rebekah," Judah said. "I'm not going to risk his life on that assumption."

"Okay," I said. "But, Judah, you can't swim. Let me go get someone who—"

"No."

"Michael's on the swim team, Judah. He could get out if he really—"

"No!" He spun around quickly in the hungry water and grabbed my arms. The fierceness in his grip and in his eyes frightened me. He was beyond reasoning with. "I'm not going to let another person die because I *assumed* he really didn't mean what he was saying," he shouted. "I'm not!"

"Judah—"

Before I could finish, he released me and forged through the water until it stole his footing. He flipped onto his stomach, put his head in the water, and paddled defiantly toward the opposite shore.

"I'm going for help," Rachel yelled, running back toward the trail.

I glanced around in disbelief. Michael was still lying like a drenched dishrag over the gleaming corner of a rock. And Judah was . . . where *was* Judah?

Without thinking, I flung myself headfirst into the water. It tugged at me, twisted me, forced itself into my mouth and lungs; chilled me, terrified me, and finally, mercifully, thrust me into a boulder. Clawing desperately at the rock, I pulled myself up. My arms and lungs were burning, and each breath tore at my throat. I rubbed my eyes and looked downstream. I saw Judah a lot farther downstream than where Michael should have been. I couldn't see Michael anywhere.

Shaking, I stood and leaped onto shore. Once I reached the spot where I knew Michael had been lying and still failed to see him, I grew frightened. The currents around these boulders pushed and ripped at each other, and could easily trap a body—injured or not—under water.

I waved to Judah, who had established a tentative hold on a boulder, and shouted, "Where's Michael?"

Lowering his head, he pointed with his left hand toward the trees behind me.

"Enjoy your swim, Cahill? Energizing, isn't it?"

"You *jerk*," I spat silently at Michael. He was fine. Drying, even. Standing on both legs. Grinning.

I looked past him at Judah. Beside the boulder he was clinging to were a few more boulders in foaming, splashing water. Beyond them—just beyond—the canyon narrowed and the river became furious, snarling, greedy water battling huge stone pillars on its way to the calm below.

I hurried toward Judah, forgetting Michael for now, and stepped back into the water several feet upstream from him. The water here was deceptively still. Strong currents swept around smaller rocks beneath the surface, making a steady foothold impossible. My ankles twisted in its pressure. I crept forward until I knew the next step would be stolen from me. "You okay?" I asked Judah.

Slowly he nodded. "Aside from being stupid, you mean?"

I could barely hear him, but I could tell by the bulge of the veins in his neck that he had shouted. The roar of the rapids beyond us overpowered everything. I wanted to tell him that he had done the good thing. That he'd acted heroically, even if somewhat irrationally. That I was proud of him. But he would never hear me and would probably not believe me anyway. "Judah, I'm going to get you out safe," I yelled. "I promise."

After glancing at the water between us, then up at me, he shook his head. "No, Rebekah. Don't. Wait—"

I surrendered myself to the river while he was still speaking. He would freeze in this water before someone else got here to help him out. I was confident in my ability to rescue him, but the current quickly proved that I had overestimated myself. It yanked me immediately off course and smashed me into a boulder . . . under the water. Pinned and held me there. I pulled frantically downward with my arms and tried to lower my feet to the bottom, but the water refused to release me. It pressed me against the rock again. It hurt, my bones slamming into rock and being squeezed by so many pounds of moving water.

I couldn't breathe.

I could hear the pounding of my heart. The pulsing of blood in my veins.

My lungs tightened.

Everything was going black.

But not fast enough. If I didn't inhale, I would explode.

Cold, cold water.

I clutched at the surface again. Again it denied me.

Just as it occurred to me to watch for the replay of my life, something squeezed my arm and I was up and out.

"Rebekah? Rebekah!"

Judah.

I leaned weakly into him, coughing and gasping.

"She okay?"

Michael. He actually sounded concerned.

I nodded.

"She's okay," Judah yelled.

"Hurry and get out," Michael ordered. "You two idiots are making me nervous."

Judah held me until my breathing relaxed to almost normal, and then a little longer.

"Come on," Michael urged from shore. "Get out!"

"Like it's so easy!" I shouted, angry at Michael's impatience when it was *his* prank that had gotten us into this danger. "Any suggestions?"

He looked at me as if I were stupid. "Swimming comes to mind."

Will he never quit?

"You know Judah can't swim!"

His grin turned uncertain and then disappeared. "He can't?" The sudden fear in his eyes convinced me that he really hadn't known.

But it didn't matter. This was still his fault.

"Michael?" Judah pointed toward a thick cluster of gnarled tree roots. "Any long sticks in there, Michael?"

Michael vanished for a moment and returned with a three-inch thick tree limb a few inches taller than himself. He jumped confidently to the third rock from shore and stretched it out toward us.

"Okay." Judah squeezed my arm. "I'm going to hold onto your hand. You're going to hold onto this rock. I'll step out and grab the stick, and Hercules over there will pull us in. Sound okay?"

Terrified, but aware of our lack of options, I consented. The force of the current tugged at Judah as soon as he stepped away from the rock. I stretched as far as I dared, as did he, but he could not reach the stick. Michael leaned toward us and nearly toppled from his rock.

"Be careful, Michael," I shouted. "Fall in there and you're in the rapids. I'd hate to see even you at the other end of that." I smiled, but without joy or humor.

This water would not forgive even the slightest error.

Michael held the stick out again.

Judah leaned to reach it, loosening his grip on my hand. Not much, but enough for the current. It snatched his legs out from under him and pushed him fully into the water, face first. Its pressure spun him toward the rapids and fought to claim him.

I tightened my grip on his hand and willed myself to hold on . . . *hold on* . . . while he attempted to regain his footing.

Michael leaped back to shore. He ran through thick snarls of tree roots and hopped onto a small boulder just behind Judah. "Let him go, Becky!" He held out the stick.

"No!" Tears—and water splashing off the rock—nearly blinded me. "No!"

"You're going to get pulled in too! Let him go!"

"No!"

But while I tried to strengthen my grip, Judah made his hand limp in mine and it slipped easily from my grasp. Without resistance from me, the river pulled him mercilessly toward the churning white rapids.

I screamed.

Only Michael stood between Judah and certain injury—or death.

Michael Kramer.

"Judah? Open your eyes, man!" Michael lay atop the last boulder before the fiercest rapids, holding the stick out about a foot above the water. "Grab the stick, Ewen! It's right behind you . . . *NOW!*"

Judah lifted his hands and grabbed the stick. He held it, but the current dragged his legs around, twisting him until he was clinging to its tip only, and most of his body was hanging in white water.

"Hold on, man!" Michael planted his toes into a crack in the rock and rose to his knees, trying to maneuver for better support. But he slipped. The current and Judah's weight on the end of the stick yanked him onto his stomach—hard—before he was able to slow its momentum. "Hold on, Ewen! I've got you, man!"

I had to do something. I had to get to Michael and help him pull Judah in. I had to.

I let go of the rock. I paddled, fought, and—only with God's help, I was sure—found myself pressed against Michael's boulder and pulling on his shoes to drag myself up. I crawled up beside him, shivering, and wrapped my hands around the stick. We pulled. Bark clawed at my palms, making them bleed, but I didn't feel it.

"It's going to work," I shouted. "Hang on, Judah, we're almost—"

Something I barely noticed from the corner of my eye snapped my head around.

"Michael!"

His hands were cut and bleeding. His face was screaming in the anguish of the fight and in fear of the consequences should he lose it. "Just pull," he yelled.

"Michael, look—"

But it was too late.

A fallen tree, like a battering ram in the current, smacked into Judah. Its roots entangled and imprisoned his arms, and dragged him forward and under. The stick ripped through our hands before slapping against the rock and hitting the water with an inaudible splash.

"He's going to die in there! He's going over the rapids! He's going to—" I collapsed, so numb in heart and body that I couldn't even cry.

Then I looked at Michael.

"This is your fault!" I shouted, hating him. Hating him. "He's going to *die,* and it's *your* fault."

He bolted from the rock and jumped toward shore.

"Where are you going?" Every muscle in my body had locked itself around my hatred. "What are you doing?"

"We've got to get to the bottom. Maybe he'll be okay, Becky. We've got to . . . to get down there."

Was he crying?

I didn't care.

I followed him, hopping from rock to rock to rock to shore, so cold that my legs felt like wet bags of dirt. I began to cry and scream, hurling accusations at Michael until he spun around on the edge of a jagged outcropping above the rapids.

"Shut up!" he screamed back. Tear trails streaked his flushed and dirty face. "You think I need someone to tell me? I know whose fault this is! I know! Okay? But . . . if we're going to get him out of this, we're going to do it together. Yell at me all you want . . . later. For now, just . . . just *shut up!*"

I did.

Michael led me through rocks, twisted wood, and a long and perilous stretch of the almost-vertical canyon wall. Finally we reached the bottom of the rapids where a wide spot in the canyon slowed the river. I did not know how long we had struggled through nature to reach this quiet place, except that it seemed too long.

"I don't see him, Michael."

It seemed dark. Towering rock shaded the water from the brilliant sunlight. On any other day, this place would have been restful. Today it was only cold.

Michael ran to a log that lay trapped between two boulders in the shallow water near the shore. He stopped when he got there and stepped back with a ragged, indrawn gasp. "Here, Becky."

I forced my legs to run to him.

Behind the log, tangled in its branches, lay Judah, completely submerged in the still water.

"Help me get him out," Michael whispered.

"He's dead. He's—"

"Help me get him out!"

I stepped close and tugged at Judah's arms until the branches released them. Then we freed his legs, one of which had snapped just below the knee. His hair was stuck to the left side of his head in matted red-brown clumps. His skin was as colorless as the water which had smothered his life—and as cold. His lips were blue. When we dragged him to shore, he felt heavy. Lifeless. I sank to the dirt and cradled him against my chest.

No pulse.

Michael pulled him quickly away from me and laid him on his back. He tilted Judah's head back, pinched his nostrils shut, breathed twice into his open mouth, and began administering first-aid CPR. He counted to five. Three times. Two more breaths.

"Michael, tell me what to do. I don't know CPR."

Another breath. "Talk to him."

I swiped at tears with hands I could no longer feel. "What? What will that do?"

"Just do it!"

I did, whenever Michael wasn't at Judah's face, breathing.

Fight with us, Judah. Don't die. Breathe. Please breathe. We're here, Judah. Don't give up. We love you. I love you. Breathe.

I talked and cried. Michael worked.

Whenever water rose in Judah's mouth, Michael rolled him gently onto his side to dispel it, checked for a pulse, grimaced, and began again.

Time seemed to halt as Michael counted to five again and again. He looked to be tiring when I heard a shout from upstream.

"They're coming, Michael," I said. I jumped up and rushed into the water to see clearly. "It's Nathan!"

"It won't matter." Michael's voice was weary—sapped of courage. "He's not coming back."

Even as I urged him, begged him, not to give up, Judah's stillness contended with my stubborn hope. His unresponsive body appeared as lifeless as the soaked sweatshirt hanging from my shoulders.

Nathan stumbled down the slope, splashed into the river and past me to his brother. He yanked Michael aside and continued CPR himself. Between breaths and compressions, he said, "Michael, run back and tell them what's happened. Tell them to send someone for help. Rebekah, come over here and take his wet shoes and socks off. He's cold."

Exhausted, Michael and I obeyed without thought, passing by each other in the river.

I reached out and touched Michael's shoulder.

He kept walking as if he hadn't noticed.

"Come on, Judah, *Fight!*" Nathan's face tightened with each compression of Judah's chest until he could no longer contain his emotion. "Why'd you jump in there for . . . *him?* He didn't . . . deserve that." He shook his head and resumed counting under his breath. "I'm sorry, Judah." Two breaths. "I mean it. I'm sorry. *Fight.*"

I began cutting at Judah's jersey with the pocket knife Nathan tossed to me.

"Breathe, Judah," Nathan yelled into his brother's face. "Breathe!"

As if Judah had heard and was trying to obey, a forceful stream of water exploded from his mouth.

Nathan stopped at three-one-thousand to roll him onto his side. When he pushed him back, pressing two fingers at Judah's Adam's apple, he signalled me with a flick of his wrist. "Breathe twice for me," he said. " I think I've got a pulse! Pinch his nose."

I did.

More water.

"Again, Rebekah."

I did.

"Give me your hand." When I reached out to him, Nathan grabbed my fingers and held them tightly against Judah's throat. "Anything?"

I could barely feel it. A slow, distant, not quite even beating. But it was persistent. "Is that him?"

"That's him. Breathe again."

I smiled and began to cry. "Thank God."

"We're not there yet," Nathan cautioned me quietly. "Breathe again."

I did.

The others came. Dad. Pastor Ewen. Mr. Kramer. Mr. Dunn. They covered Judah in their jackets and sweatshirts while Mrs. Potts, a nurse, took over his care.

"They're sending for a helicopter," Dad told me, pulling me down to the ground beside him and holding me tight in his warm arms. "They'll do everything they can."

I nodded, knowing, as I heard Mrs. Potts say, "I've lost his pulse, Ben," that that might not be enough.

I was so tired. So cold in my still-wet clothes. So numbed from everything that had happened. My eyes were burning, but I didn't want to close them because when I did—

Black . . . gray . . . white . . . Judah sitting on the curb at our church parking lot, sunlight in his tidy brown hair and life in his blue-gray eyes, folding the bulletin and smiling at me.

Don't die, Judah.

Chapter Twenty

"They're here, Beck."

My fingers tingled as I snapped a clip into my hair.

A red blur, Mom swooshed into the room, closed the door, and hugged me. "Judah looks good today," she said. "I can't believe how quickly he's getting back to normal."

I laughed. A broken leg, two cut-up hands, twenty stitches, and a huge bruise behind his left ear; easy breathlessness and ribs that protested every movement hardly constituted *normal*. But he was getting there.

A healthy brown had begun to reclaim his face. His eyes had their curious spark again. His mind—and brain—were well and functioning. That had been a strangling concern during his thirty-eight hours of unconsciousness at the hospital. *When he wakes up—if he wakes up—will he be able to speak? See? Remember who he is? Who I am?*

Checking my hair in the mirror, I pushed the memory of those hours of terrible waiting from my mind. "He's a miracle. What can I tell you?"

"Sure is."

I followed my mother into the living room, where Dad was insisting to Judah that he really should sit down, and Judah was quietly declining. Greeting Judah with a gentle squeeze of his elbow, I smiled at Dad. "It probably hurts him more to sit down and get back up again than it does to just stand there."

Judah's grin did not erase the seriousness in his eyes. "Are you ready?" he asked me, readjusting his grip on his crutches.

I frowned at Rachel, who was standing near the front door, and then at Dad. "Are you sure you want to do this today, Judah? You just got out of the hos—"

"I'm sure."

"Okay," I said, shrugging. "Then I'm ready too."

Rachel and I helped Judah into her little car, and we were off to look for Michael Kramer.

"I called Mr. Kramer this morning." I leaned forward and rested my hand on Judah's shoulder. "He said Michael has been spending a lot of time flying his helicopter at that field on Wilkens Road."

"We'll go there first," he said. "Do you know the road, Rachel?"

"Yep."

Rachel looked about as pleased to be on this mission as someone leading the police to her errant cousin's drug operation. Undoubtedly, she considered Michael's battle with guilt and his resulting withdrawal from everyone—including his parents, insufficient punishment for him. I did. But, like me, she loved her brother. So, here we were, cruising along Wilkens Road in search of the boy who had destroyed her father's pastorate and had nearly done the same to Judah.

"What will you say to him if he is there?" she asked Judah.

"That I forgive him." He pointed out his window at the golden pink sky. "There's a little plane. And a helicopter."

I smiled as Judah watched the brightly painted miniatures in delight. The two remote-controlled planes and one helicopter in the air were spectacular to watch, but I was much more captivated by Judah's boyish appreciation of them.

Until we pulled to a stop in the unpaved parking lot, next to Michael's black pickup.

"Do you want me to go with you?" Rachel asked.

"No." He unfastened his seat belt, struggled to coax his crutches out the door, then grabbed the top of his door and started to pull himself up.

"He won't accept it," Rachel said. "Your forgiveness. I mean, would you have, if Mr. Cook had offered it to you?"

Judah sat down again and shook his head. "Not then." He stared at his sister. "I would now, though."

"Yeah, well, he has nothing to forgive you for." When she turned to face him after rolling down her window, Rachel's expression revealed her undecided reaction to Judah's admission. Was she relieved that he might finally be willing to receive forgiveness and move on? Or was she frustrated with his continued unwillingness to let go of his perceived responsibility in Tommy's death? It was impossible to tell.

"Maybe not," Judah said, "but I'd take it, all the same." He glanced over his shoulder at me. "What you said that day on Bethel

Road is probably right. I'm not the person to help someone out of danger in a river. Still . . . I don't know." Shuddering, he added, "I could have gotten you or Michael hurt, Rebekah, because fear and wanting to make right kept me from using my brain. Michael may have provoked me, but I made my own decision about getting in that water. What happened to me isn't totally his fault. I want him to understand that, because I know how he feels right now."

"But Judah—"

"I know, Rachel. Let's just . . . pray, okay?"

When Judah prayed aloud that Michael would receive his forgiveness and return to his normal self, I added the silent correction that Michael would return to us slightly or significantly refined.

Rachel and I watched silently as Judah approached the picnic table where Michael was refuelling his green and white miniature helicopter. He greeted him, admired his machine, and sat beside him on the bench to talk with him for nearly an hour.

"Poor Michael," I muttered absently when I saw him bury his face in his hands for the second time.

Rachel squinted at me. "Poor *Michael?*"

After studying the anger in her eyes and glancing again at Michael, I decided to defend my thought. "Think how tough it must be for him, Rachel. He did all that horrible junk to Judah, and then Judah was willing to jump into a wild river, when he can't even swim, to help him out. Who could live with that?"

"He should have thought of that before Judah got near the water. Judah could have died, Rebekah. Almost did. All I can see when I look at Michael is the kid who is responsible. You have to understand that. Judah might be willing to forgive him, but I don't think I am. And Michael did a lot more to us than just what happened at the river. I won't accuse him to his face, or hate him to other people behind his back because I saw what Judah went through with that. But . . . in my heart?" She shook her head. "I know it's wrong of me, and I'm trying, but he . . ."

"Trust me, Rachel," I said, reaching between the two front seats to clasp her hand, "I understand."

"I know you do."

"Michael is really messed up inside. Maybe some good will come out of this for him."

Rachel nodded. "Maybe. Too late for Dad, though, but . . . maybe."

"And, Rachel," I said gently, "if Michael hadn't started CPR when he did, Judah—"

"I know." She stayed quiet a long time, staring first at the steering wheel and then out at Michael. "Then there's Jesus' example. How much He has already forgiven us . . . and will be ready to forgive us in our lifetime." Raising her hand to her eyes, she admitted, "It's tough, though. Real hard."

"Yeah. It is."

When Judah returned to the car a few minutes later, he looked discouraged, wearied.

"How'd it go?" I asked him.

"He wouldn't say too much." He pulled his door shut and allowed Rachel to fasten his seat belt. "Now I know why everyone felt so . . . impatient with me."

"It's hard," Rachel said, starting the car. "On both ends."

As we drove back toward town, I wondered where the Ewens would be in a week's time. Montana? Mrs. Ewen had mentioned an interest in visiting Mount Rushmore. Would they go there?

They would not be with us. That was the only certainty.

They had stayed an extra week already, and now that Judah had been released from the hospital, they were planning to leave tomorrow after church.

Tomorrow.

I denied those frustrating but increasingly common tears with the realization that wherever the Ewens ended up, heaven was a lot farther away. Judah could too easily have gone there. Reaching forward to gently squeeze his shoulder again, I thanked God for his recovery.

And for the post office.

While I still did not want letters from Montana, I felt more than convinced that they would suit me a whole lot better than a funeral card.

Chapter Twenty-One

Nathan guarded Judah the following morning at church as if he thought that the slightest touch from a curious child would further injure him. Everyone seemed to have something to say to Judah, from "We're glad you pulled through so well," to "Did you see the Great White Light before they revived you?" But Nathan allowed them only brief moments to say it. He escorted Judah hastily down the left aisle to the front row and sat him between his father and me.

In moderation meant nothing to Nathan this morning when it came to praising his brother. He had learned a thing or two about Judah—and about toughness—that day at the river, and nobody was going to enter or leave the church without hearing about it. Everyone already knew every detail of what had happened and then some, but I never interrupted Nathan to point this out.

Judah tolerated the overprotection and admiration with an attitude of relaxed humor, seeming to be genuinely relieved about being kept out of reach of so many suddenly loving hands. Certainly, Nathan's respect and approval meant more to him than whatever anyone else could have said, anyway.

But beneath the pleasantness of this Sunday morning—through and all around it—lurked a numbing sadness.

I looked past Judah at his father. "Pastor Ewen?"

Not smiling, he glanced up at me.

"I . . . I want you to know that I'm sorry you're leaving."

His expression lightened as he gently nudged Judah with his elbow. "I know you are."

"No," I pressed on, too serious to be embarrassed by his tease. "I mean I'm sad *you're* leaving. You're an excellent pastor. Don't think you're not."

A look passed between father and son that pushed aside any concern I may have been pretending to ignore about the well-being of their relationship. Then Pastor Ewen said, "I'm sad to be leaving too, Rebekah. We have real friends here."

"The best," Judah added.

Pastor Fenton stepped to the pulpit then and opened the service in prayer. Just in time. I had determined not to cry until *after* the Ewens had pulled out of the church parking lot, and Judah's quiet assertion had come very close to toppling that resolve.

Judah sat through the first half of the sermon stiffly, visibly distracted. Uninterested. This was not like him.

"What's the matter?" I leaned toward him to whisper. "Headache?"

"No." He looked over his shoulder at the doors and then back at me. "The Kramers aren't here."

I shrugged. "Can you blame them?"

"I guess not," he said, still discontent.

"Judah, they probably don't know—"

Just then, one of the entryway doors hissed open, and almost everyone turned to see who possessed the nerve to arrive so tardily—and noisily—to church.

The *Kramers* . . . though they looked anything but nervy.

Tony and Mrs. Kramer stayed in back with the ushers, but Mr. Kramer and Michael walked doggedly up the left aisle and sat in the front row—beside me.

I did not appreciate the sentiment, whatever it might have been, and slid as far away from Mr. Kramer as I could get without putting myself in Judah's lap.

All eyes turned back to Pastor Fenton, who finished his sermon in spite of the tangible and sickening tension in the sanctuary.

At the conclusion of the closing hymn, Mr. Kramer approached the platform and asked Pastor Fenton if he could speak.

Beside me, Judah shifted in his chair.

"Joe," Pastor Fenton responded, twisting his wedding band, "this isn't the way we prefer to—"

"Please, Pastor Fenton. This concerns everyone here, and I can't stand under it any longer." Mr. Kramer looked ready to cave in.

After glancing at Dad and Pastor Ewen, both of whom could only shrug, Pastor Fenton nodded and handed the microphone to Mr. Kramer.

"Ben said a couple of weeks ago that Pastor Fenton was coming here to sort out and correct problems." Mr. Kramer licked his lips and bowed his head. "I'm going to do it for him."

Papers rustled. Mothers whispered their children into silence.

"I am the problem. I correct it with my resignation."

I gasped.

"I'm not fit to be in any leadership position, least of all the one I most covet—pastor." For the first time since coming to the platform, Mr. Kramer raised his eyes enough for me to see them. They were dull. Weary. "I manipulated the board against every pastor sent here, including Ben Ewen. And with Ben, I allowed things to go beyond . . . politics. Understand, though, that the blame doesn't belong with Michael. It belongs with me. I found out what he was doing . . . and I didn't stop him. My ambition motivated him. My hunger fueled him. I failed Michael. I used him. I failed you. I used you. I must apologize. To God. To Ben. To the board. To all of you. Most of all, to Judah Ewen. I'm sorry."

I had never seen a man so broken. Should I grieve for him, or hate him? Respect his honesty, or loathe his baseness? I didn't know, and I suspected that very few of us, if anyone, did.

"Last weekend, Judah nearly drowned. Not the result of an innocent 'Help, I'm drowning' prank, but a deliberate attempt to twist the knife of Ben's dismissal. What happened was never intended, of course, but it happened. Since that day, not one of the Ewen family has accused my son or expressed any hatred toward him. Or me. I know they must feel it, and that we deserve it. Instead, they've gone out of their way to extend kindness to Michael because they know his . . . his burden. Even during those hours when Judah could as easily have died as lived—" His voice faltered. He swallowed a deep breath. "Judah . . . Judah went to Michael yesterday, first thing out of the hospital, to . . . to *forgive* him. You cannot know what that means unless you know what it is he's willing to forgive. I do know."

The anguish of the man's heart escaped through his eyes in genuine tears. "Neither Michael, nor I, can stand in our wrong in the face of that kind of forgiveness. I have to repent. I have to resign. And . . ." He straightened his shoulders, steadied his face, and looked directly at Pastor Ewen. "I have to recommend that the board seriously reconsider the pastor we just voted out. He has proven, now even more than before—in himself and in the character of the kids he's raised, that he's the best pastor we've seen—or will see—around here." As he stepped from the platform, his eyes stayed right on Pastor Ewen's. "If he'll stay."

When Mr. Kramer walked by us toward Michael, Judah grabbed his crutches and moved to stand up. Pastor Ewen laid a firm hand on his shoulder. Judah obeyed his father's stay, but I could see in his eyes as he watched the Kramers leave that he regretted denying the man an acknowledgement of his repentance.

"This isn't the place," Pastor Ewen explained when the people around us began gathering their things to leave. "I'll be sure you get a chance to see it finished."

Judah nodded.

When Pastor Ewen had left with Dad, Mr. Potts, and Pastor Fenton, I leaned back in my chair and closed my eyes. "Wow. I can't even think."

"Yeah," Judah said. "Pretty heavy."

We stayed silent awhile.

"Do you think they'll ask him to stay?" Judah asked me.

I nodded. "Do you think he will?"

"His heart's here now."

When Judah smiled and squeezed my hand, I realized not only that I could love him, and that I probably already did, but that his need had forced me to consider and strive forward in my own need for God in a way I never had before. My understanding of Christ and my relationship with Him seemed . . . no, *was* . . . more real now. More personal. More important. I suspected that Judah had gained his share of insight through all this too. He was still smiling.

"He'll stay," Judah said.

"It's because of you, y'know," I said.

He shook his head and scrunched up his face the way he always did when he thought I had exaggerated one of his attributes. "It was a start, maybe, but God's the one who changes hearts."

"I know. Still, I'm proud of you."

"I'll take that, I guess." With a grimace and a gentle boost from me, he stood, and we went to the entryway to wait for our parents.

God's the one who changes hearts.

God had changed a lot more than hearts for Judah, me, our families, and our church. Staring through the window at the warm sun, with Judah beside me, I thanked Him.

For promises kept.

And for the certainty that He wasn't done yet . . . which was an exciting promise in itself.

"Rebekah?"

I turned to face Judah. "Yeah?"

"Since we're going to be staying, there's something on my mind that I've been meaning to ask you."

"What's that?" I asked, enjoying the absence of tension in his tone—and the grin in his blue-gray eyes.

"Would you really go to New York without me?"